Aim

Skye Lotus

Skye Lotus Publishing
Melbourne, Australia

Copyright © 2014 by Skye Lotus.

All rights reserved. No part of this publication may be reproduced, distributed or transmitted in any form or by any means, including photocopying, recording, or other electronic or mechanical methods, without the prior written permission of the publisher, except in the case of brief quotations embodied in critical reviews and certain other non-commercial uses permitted by copyright law. For permission requests, write to the publisher, addressed "Attention: Permissions Coordinator," at the address below.

Skye Lotus
skye@skyelotus.com
www.skyelotus.com

Publisher's Note: This is a work of fiction. Names, characters, places, and incidents are a product of the author's imagination. Locales and public names are sometimes used for atmospheric purposes. Any resemblance to actual people, living or dead, or to businesses, companies, events, institutions, or locales is completely coincidental.

Book Layout © 2013 BookDesignTemplates.com
Cover Artwork © 2014 Maja Majetic

Ordering Information:
Quantity sales. Special discounts are available on quantity purchases by corporations, associations, and others. For details, contact the "Special Sales Department" at the address above.

Aim/ Skye Lotus. -- 1st ed.
ISBN 978-0-9925010-0-6

To Skye -
It's an awesome name, isn't it?
Kudos for sharing it with me, and thanks for
being a little ball of sunshine that I've only met
once. I think you're absolutely fabulous.

CHAPTER ONE

Reality or Dreams?

Zara looked out the window. Golden clouds masked her view. She couldn't see the green grass of the fields, or the kids playing outside with their most recent toys or gadgets. It was strange to see only glowing gold everywhere she looked...

At least, that was how she imagined it. Cut out from her dreams by her alarm clock, or rather, clocks, Zara rubbed her head drowsily and sat up, kicking her bed sheets back. Quickly, she put on her slippers of red velvet and slammed her hand down onto one alarm clock, then another, and another, until all were silent apart from their endless ticking.

It was 8:30, and it was a Saturday, which meant Zara was free to do anything she wished. Cinching a watch onto her wrist, she walked down the stairs into the kitchen, where she found her father, Sera, slicing bacon into thin strips.

"What's the special occasion?" Zara inquired, raising an eyebrow in surprise at the arrangement of food her father had made.

There was a small platter of boiled eggs and another of poached eggs, while a plate of fried and a dish of scrambled eggs were also set out on the countertop. There were pancakes, which were stacked clumsily on top of one another. Maple and golden syrup were set aside from the shiny plate, and a tub of cream joined them.

"I'm hungry, and no doubt you are too!" Sera grinned playfully, looking up from his handy knife work. He threw the bacon slices into a pan, where they started to sizzle.

"Yeah, but how are the two of us supposed to eat all that?" Zara asked, thinking her father mad.

"You know me," Sera said, patting his stomach, "I'll wipe any plate clean."

"Appetite of a God, that's what you have, Dad," Zara commented, wiping sleep from her eyes. She sat down on a swivel chair and took a plate from the counter, along with a knife and fork. "May I?"

Sera shrugged, his broad shoulders lifting up to his ears. "May as well. This bacon won't take long."

Zara smiled and poured herself a glass of orange juice. "One, two, three, four, and five..." she counted as the orange liquid poured in.

Sera shook his head. "Tut, tut, always timing things, aren't you? Maybe you should time how long it takes for me to make your breakfast. It's already been half an hour, why don't you keep track?"

Zara pursed her lips. Her father's sarcastic comment stopped her counting out loud but still she timed it in her head. Finally, the glass was full to the brim. Eleven and three quarter seconds; not bad for a late morning.

Zara shoved some things onto her plate – a couple of eggs here and there, even a pancake – but she didn't stay eating for long. Soon she was walking back up the stairs to get dressed.

"Missy, you forgot your glass of orange juice!" Sera called after her, but she didn't take any notice. She had left it there on purpose. A test. Just a test.

Zara found a brush and tried pulling it through her knotted hair, but found it got stuck. She gave up and picked an outfit from her wardrobe and slipped the clothes on, counting under her breath how long it took. She found herself looking at her black leather jacket in disgust, as it had wrinkles and creases all over it. She pulled it on reluctantly and zipped up her boots.

When Zara reached her bathroom mirror, she found herself staring at a completely tidy young girl, as if she had never had her hair scrunched up or been wearing her scruffy jacket. The jacket was clean and smooth, with no creases, and her hair was curled perfectly into bouncy ringlets that framed her pale face. But she was used to it. It happened every morning.

Quickly, she glanced out the window. It was sunny and bright, and lots of kids were out playing street cricket. She longed to join them. One day, she would. She had never been outside before, and it was her dearest wish to.

Zara skipped down the stairs two at a time. "Dad, can I go outside today? It looks all sunny and bright, surely I can go and see some people?"

Sera frowned, finishing off the last pancake. The glass of orange juice was empty, and all of the eggs, slices of bacon and toast had disappeared; the only traces left of them were crumbs. "Not today, missy. No, definitely not today. Bad weather. You don't want to go out there today."

Zara sighed. "But it looks so nice! How can those rays of sunshine indicate bad weather?"

"Not another word about it, young missy. I'm not having you baked dry like an autumn leaf out there. Now, find something else to do, like draw or watch TV," Sera said sternly, his tone changing in an instant.

Zara was sick of doing both those activities. But she crossed her arms and trudged out into the living room, where the couch and TV beckoned. She rolled her eyes and looked over at her drawing desk. It was covered in pages and pages of designs, outfits, and beautiful faces.

Zara decided to count the hours of television she could watch without getting bored. That wouldn't last very long, but she had other things to count too. She picked up a remote and the screen flickered on. White noise exploded from the speakers. She sat down and surfed the channels, already feeling restless.

"What should I do once I've counted everything in this house? There'll be nothing left to do, and I'm not allowed outside at all. Maybe I could count how many times I can do everything over and over again..." Zara whispered, going into the counting trance she had been in many times before. As her eyes unfocused, she caught a glimpse of Sera standing in the doorway holding a phone to his ear. Then everything went blurry, then finally, black.

Sera turned away from Zara who was now staring into the screen of the TV. He felt his phone buzz, and snapped it open and held it against his ear.

"Hello, Ares, God of War speaking. If this is a prank, I'll send you a spear and a warrior."

A voice crackled to life at the other end of the line. "You needn't be so threatening, Ares, it's just me." The voice sounded sweet and friendly, if a little high pitched.

Sera's face softened immediately. "Aphrodite, what are you doing, calling when Zara could be close by?"

There was a soft sigh at the other end. "But she's not, is she? Otherwise you would not have mentioned my name aloud. Your strategy is much too predictable, Ares."

Sera felt a surge of anger flow through him. "My strategies are the best! Especially in battle—"

There was a screech of laughter at the other end. "And far too easy to anger, Ares. Relax, I was only joking with you. Now, don't go insulting Athena. She is called Goddess of Battle Strategy and Wisdom for a reason, you know."

Sera calmed down a little, but now he was on guard. "Why are you calling? Zara could snap out of her trance any moment. She can't know about us, or the others! It's suicide giving that away to her!"

"I think it's time you let her outside."

"What? No! She cannot know! It is far too dangerous," Sera yelled, suddenly panicking.

"She can't be cooped up like this forever, Ares. She will escape one day from your cruel imprisonment. She is a minor Goddess. It is her will to break free." Suddenly, there was a clicking noise, and the call was cut off.

Sera threw the phone on the floor and jumped on top of it, smashing it to pieces. "I will not be ordered around by a Goddess! I will not tolerate it!"

No sooner had he said this but another voice filled his ears. "Dad, what? A Goddess? Are you feeling okay?" Zara was standing up, poised stiffly. "If you're having a hyper again, sit down on the floor and wait till I get a paper bag."

Sera shook his head at his own foolishness. "No, it's not that. I got a call from someone, that's all."

Zara frowned. "Don't lie. What is this 'Goddess' business? Why did you smash the phone? Answer!" Suddenly, Zara's similarity to Sera stood out as her voice turned to stone and became commanding. With her black sunglasses atop her head, she looked all the part.

Sera rubbed his head wearily. "Please, all these questions are a little far-fetched. Just go back to watching TV, okay?"

Zara looked furious. "TV! Draw! Do anything but be curious! For once, I am going outside! I am going to be sun burnt or soaked, cold or hot. I will feel what it is really like to be human!"

Sera cocked his head in confusion. "But I thought you liked those things. You draw such nice pictures, and the TV always has something on."

Zara switched on the TV and glared at Sera angrily. "I have seen it all before. Nothing in this house is interesting except counting everything over and over again!"

Throwing the remote on the floor, Zara made her way towards the front door.

"Don't go outside, Zara. It's not safe," Sera warned, his voice a deep, throaty rumble.

Zara turned back to him, her hand on the knob. Like lightning, her hand turned round and the door swung open. It looked as it did out the window; all natural, green and grassy, with houses lining the streets.

"I have never been outside before. That changes today," Zara claimed triumphantly, her head lifted defiantly.

Then, after her moment of power, she stepped out the door.

CHAPTER TWO

Discovery and Secrets

As soon she laid her foot on the concrete, her outer vision changed. All the houses disappeared, the grass vaporised and the black rubble of the road fell away into nothing. Instead, golden clouds stretched out for miles, and silver bridges that shone brightly led over gaps in the clouds. Zara held her breath with shock and stepped forwards again.

The silver paving under her foot did not waver, so it was not an illusion. It was very solid, too, and it did not fall out from beneath her. A golden tower she could see in the distance was glowing invitingly. Quickly, she sped up and started crossing bridges to get closer to it.

She could hear Sera running after her, yelling warnings and threats. She did not falter, but increased her quick pace with eagerness. The bridges gleamed as soon as she stepped onto them, and directed her to-wards the tower.

As she went, she noticed that some other silver paths led off to different areas; a forest of opalescent trees, a lake of crystalline water and darker areas off through more storm-like clouds.

When she reached the large double doors of the tower, she finally looked back. The house that she had come from had changed into what looked like a war-plane. It hovered in mid-air over a mass of golden clouds. She could see Sera now, and he was stuck at a bridge crossing where a plank of the silver wood had fallen away.

Turning back to the castle, she pushed open the doors. A small room led to a spiral staircase, which twisted upwards into a somewhat darker domain. Has-tily, Zara started to run up the stairs, eager to see where they would take her. Somehow, the darkness beckoned for her to come forth and present herself.

The stairs led a long way up, and when Zara reached the top she felt a little out of breath. It was pitch black, apart from a glowing orb that spat out bolts of electricity every few seconds. It was contained in a glass case, which hovered in the air, and it didn't look as if it was about to drop down.

And then lights turned on, bright and blinding. Zara winced and shut her eyes tightly, then she opened them and looked around.

A man as tall a lamppost was looking down on her, his face a picture of bewilderment. He was wearing a black work shirt and a pair of azure jeans. His hair was tousled and walnut brown, and his eyes were chemical blue. He held a spear in his right hand, which was bright white and hard to look at without squinting. He exuded an aura of power and importance.

"Who are you?" the man's loud voice echoed around the room. Zara had only just realised how high the roof was, and how big the doorway the man had come through was. It was all very king-sized, especially the man himself.

Zara found it hard to find her voice. "Uh... I'm Zara."

The man looked back at her disbelievingly. "What is your title?"

Zara was now confused. "My title? I'm not a book, you know."

The man now seemed aggravated. "Do not speak to me in such a manner!"

Zara backed off a little, holding up her hands defensively. "Gee, big man. Sorry."

The tall man now bent down and aimed to swat at her, but Zara pointed at him sternly, right between the eyes. "If you touch me you'll regret it. I'll call my dad, Sera, and even though he's smaller than you, he'll snap your back like a twig."

The man's eyebrows shot up and his eyes blazed with fire. He was infuriated. "You dare threaten me, lesser being of the lower Earth?"

Zara lifted her head defiantly. "I do dare because I'm not afraid of you. Did you expect me to fall to the ground and tremble in fear?" she snapped back, glaring at the giant distastefully.

The big man took a great breath and tried to stop the boiling rage that was contorting his face. "What is your title?!" he asked again, more forcefully this time.

Zara looked around when she heard pounding footsteps behind her, and Sera appeared at the top of the stairs.

Only he was different. Much taller, in fact about as tall as the giant before her. He looked different, too. His arms were heavily muscled and there were a pair of gigantic black sunglasses guarding his eyes. A large tattoo ran up his left arm, with arrows, swords, spears and maces. His face was firmer, with less room for emotion. He was staring at the other man, expressionless.

"I apologise, O Zeus, for this child's arrogance and ignorance. She knows nothing of you, or of any of the other Gods or Goddesses. She is reckless and ruthless, Zeus, I deeply apologise–" Sera spluttered, approaching the other man he called Zeus.

Zeus put up his hand. "No more excuses, Ares. You could make a hundred and I would still fry this 'arrogant and ignorant' infant with my bolt. What is her title?"

Zara glanced at Sera and he looked shocked and even more worried than before. "Zara, Goddess of... well, I'm not sure yet, Zeus, she hasn't revealed her title. All I know is that her name is Zara."

Zeus looked surprised. "Has not revealed her title? That is unnatural."

Sera nodded in agreement. "Yes. She escaped, you see, because she was supposed to stay in the warplane, my domain, for her immortal life, but she... was restless. I could not stop her."

Zeus's expression softened slightly. "Curiosity killed the cat, did it not?" he said, looking down on Zara, who was biting her tongue with the effort to stay quiet.

"Please. My title? Goddess? Immortal life? You haven't told me about any of this, Dad!" Zara exclaimed, finally bursting.

Sera looked down at her, his usual look of fondness gone. "Ares, Zara. Not Dad. Ares, God of War."

Zara looked back at him angrily. "Answer."

Zeus laughed softly. "Bold, isn't she? At first I thought she was from Earth, and she somehow got up here, but now you have arrived, she is self-explanatory."

Zara now switched her focus to Zeus. "And you. You will put that stupid white spear away, get to normal size and answer for my father, if he won't himself. He's such a coward!"

To Zara's surprise, Zeus obliged. He placed the bolt down on the ground and, as he did so, he shrunk in size. But before he could open his mouth to speak, another giant of a man came up the stairs and walked into the room.

This man was wearing an ocean blue singlet top and a pair of deep blue board shorts. His eyes were soft and friendly, and smooth blue. He held a trident of crystal in his left hand, and a large pair of sandals flopped against the floor. He smiled when he saw Zara, and knelt down until his face was level with hers.

"What a little starfish you have here, Ares! Glows with confidence in the dark, too, I'll bet," he said fondly, smoothing Zara's hair back with a single finger. Zara swatted his finger away sharply, and the man's hand retreated back. "Feisty as well. Maybe that's not such a good thing."

Zeus rolled his eyes and picked up his spear of white again. Instantly he grew to the size of the others. "Poseidon. Always the first to make a good impression on someone."

The man called Poseidon closed his eyes. "The waves will soothe and befriend, whilst lightning will frighten and scatter," he recited, a mocking smile twisting his lips.

Zeus frowned. "Do not be so arrogant, Poseidon. We are at a time where we decide whether this... untitled girl lives in her immortality, or finds her way to Tartarus."

Poseidon smiled wider and opened his eyes. "I vote she lives, Zeus. I do not see the danger in another Goddess being greeted into our world."

Ares jumped in. "The danger is her ruthlessness, Poseidon. She will do whatever she can to get what she wants. Imagine the lure the power of the Master Bolt, your Crystal Trident and Hades' Helm of Shadows will have for one without even knowledge of herself."

A small trembling rumbled underneath them, and another man stepped out of the shadows of the far wall. "You dare utter my name, Ares. Why do you summon me?"

This man was all in black, with a shadowed helmet over his face. He pulled it off, revealing a young, handsome face with black, slick hair with spiked, uneven ends falling over his ears. His eyes were a rich red, and the helmet had intricate engravings in Greek.

The man stared at Zara when he realised she was there. "You best answer that girl's questions right now, Zeus, or she will bring her rage down on you, and it might just be as heavy as the sky itself," the man smiled thinly, and walked over to beside Zara, who shifted uncomfortably. His aura was strong and whispered of spirits, dead and alive. His face looked slightly sinister, and she didn't like the way he was staring at her, his eyes alight with greed.

Zeus looked down at Zara as if he had forgotten she was there. "Oh, yes, of course. Ask away, small one."

"What is going on? Why are you so big and tall? Why do you have such... unnecessarily complicated names? Who am I? What is this Crystal Trident, Master Bolt and Helmet of Shadows? Are you illusions? Am I dreaming?" Zara asked, her questions flowing like water.

Zeus laughed. "You are certainly not dreaming, and we are most definitely not illusions. Our names are those of the Greek Gods, and we are big and tall because we are Gods. The Master Bolt is my weapon of power, the Crystal Trident is the toy of Poseidon, my first brother, which he wields to make waves." At this Poseidon punched Zeus on the arm, annoyed. "And the Helmet of Shadows belongs to Hades, my youngest brother. It's a device for, let's see, melding into the shadows. Mind you, he could already do that before he put it on." Hades' eyes flashed darkly and his face went deeply serious. "And as for who you are, untitled one, we do not know. Not yet, at least."

Ares' forehead was now beaded with sweat. "Do not take her for my child, Zeus, for she is not. Aphrodite told me to take care of her when she found her sleeping in a bird's abandoned nest, although I am not quite sure I believe her story. I do not know why she took a liking to her, either."

Zeus nodded thoughtfully, rubbing his chin. "She does have quite a likeness to Aphrodite, doesn't she? The exact same chiselled face. Pretty jade eyes, too. And she is feisty, like you, Ares. I wonder what else she will reveal?"

Zara now looked up at the Gods in disappointment. "So no one knows who I am."

Hades smiled, his eyes darkening sinisterly. "I don't know, small one. I would tell you if I could, but," he paused, thinking it over, "wouldn't that ruin the story you will tell?"

Zara knitted her brows in confusion. "I don't understand, Hades. What is this 'title' business?"

Hades looked surprised. "Zeus, my oldest brother, has the title of Lord of the Sky, Ruler of Clouds and Controller of Lightning. Poseidon, my second oldest brother, has the title of Lord of the Sea, Wielder of Water, Earth Shaker and Ruler of Horses. I, Hades, the youngest of the three topmost Gods, have the title of Ruler of the Dead, King of Ghosts and Controller of Death. That last one is untrue. The Fates will organise that all for me," he drawled, clutching his helmet tightly.

Zeus, Poseidon, and Ares had been in their own conversation, but now they broke off to listen to Hades speak. "Zeus has the Master Bolt, his weapon of choice.

With it he controls where lightning strikes, when, and even upon whom in rare cases. Poseidon carries the Crystal Trident, which he uses to create waves, or tsunamis when he's upset, and move the water to the motion of the moon, which he told Artemis he would do for her. I hold my Helm of Shadows, which lets me become invisible, speak to the spirits and raise the dead, although I have never attempted it because of all the evil it would bring down on Earth."

Zeus rolled his eyes. "Who cares about this Earth beneath us? It is not important."

Hades looked hurt. "I, for one, care about my domain, and its residents above. Pan, as well. And Earth guards the depths of Tartarus. I need say no more."

Zeus nodded. "We will speak no more of this. The girl shall go to Artemis. She will stay in her care from now on."

Hades opened his mouth to protest. "But... she could come with me. She is the only person I could ever see as a successful apprentice... please, Zeus–"

Zeus held up a hand to silence him. "No one will ever be your apprentice, Hades. I forbid it. I will not let you influence a new Goddess with your black magic. She would come out... biased by your opinion."

Hades' face dropped, then he regained his composure and slid his helmet on. "I will return. And I will get my way."

And he disappeared, melting out of sight. But Zara could still see him clear as day, but obviously the other Gods in the room could not, for they turned away and began to speak again. Hades stared at Zara for quite a while, until she felt extremely uncomfortable.

Zara shivered. "Stop looking at me like that."

Hades blinked in astonishment. "How can you see me?"

"I can feel your presence, therefore I can see you," Zara answered, as if it were obvious.

Hades' smile lingered on his lips again. "It is a shame to miss out on such a worthy apprentice. Not many can sense souls." He then walked out of the room, looking very disappointed.

Zara turned away. She didn't want to watch him go, as he was frightening her a little. She saw Zeus raise his bolt and let out a spark of electricity. She frowned. What had the point of that been?

A voice behind her cut through the air so sharply that Zara nearly jumped. "You call, O Zeus, my father. What is your wish?"

Zara turned with the Gods to see who had spoken. A tall, slender woman with flowing brown hair held a bow in her right hand, and had a quiver of arrows slung over her shoulder. Her hair was braided with silver twine in some places, and a small tiara decorated with a crescent moon and stars sat upon her head. She was dressed in a long dress of aqua blue that went right to her feet. A wolf sat at her side, its golden eyes glowing.

"Artemis. I thank you for coming. I have a Godling I wish you to train," Zeus said casually.

Artemis, who stood straighter at the mention of her name, flinched when she heard 'Godling'. "A boy? Please no, dealing with my brother is hard enough."

Poseidon chuckled. "You really are set against men, aren't you?"

Artemis' facial expression turned gravely serious. "In every way, Uncle, in every way."

Zeus pointed at Zara. "You will take her to your forest and train her for the next week. Bring her back here on the last day of her training and present her skills to me. I want to be impressed. Now leave me."

Artemis eyed Zara with a glint of suspicion. "She is young. Why? What is her title?"

Zeus now pointed at the steep staircase. "Go."

Artemis sighed and motioned for Zara to follow her. Artemis sped down the stairs at such a pace Zara found it a little hard to keep up. Every time she lagged behind the wolf stopped and turned to look at her, as if he wanted to encourage her. At last, they reached the bottom and stepped out onto the golden clouds.

Artemis now slowed and stepped gracefully over the silver bridges. She turned off to the side where the opalescent trees grew. Zara followed hastily, intrigued by the glittering leaves of the trees and the inviting darkness that lurked within.

"Here you will shoot targets, sprint down the forest tracks and hunt my sacred animals, the stag, bear, snake and deer. If you find a wolf, befriend it and keep it as your partner. I advise you not to search for a man to accompany you for the rest of your life. Wolves are more loyal, and less arrogant."

The wolf at her side raised its head proudly, its black and white fur gleaming. "Astra is a perfect example," Artemis explained, scratching his ears. "He will never leave me, even after death."

Zara cocked her head to the side. "I thought you were immortal?"

Artemis nodded. "I am. But I can still die. Just... disappear, you might say, if I feel I have lost everything I stand for. But I am far too strong for that."

Zara smiled. She quite liked Artemis. "Where will I find a wolf?"

Artemis smiled back. "Anywhere in my sacred forest. Why, already plenty want to be your partner. They are watching you right now."

And just then, a wolf leapt out of the bushes. It pranced over to Zara, wagging its tail eagerly. Its fur was pure black, with a white star on its forehead. Its eyes were crimson, and Zara stared into them with interest.

"Take her. She wanted you most," Artemis insisted.

Zara nodded happily. "I'll call her..."

The wolf looked up at her, its eyes shining with anticipation.

"Yes?" Artemis asked keenly.

"Desdemona. Yes, Desdemona will be your name," Zara said clearly, rubbing the wolf's head.

Artemis recoiled a little. "If that is what her name is to be, so be it."

The wolf now called Desdemona howled softly in approval, and sat down tamely.

"Now, time to shoot," announced Artemis, and with that, she threw Zara a quiver of arrows and a bow.

CHAPTER THREE

Heaven and Hell

Artemis spent hours with Zara teaching her to shoot accurately. Zara did this speedily, and she soon was getting bull's-eyes every time. Desdemona sat beside her patiently, watching each arrow fly past and hit each target pinned to the trees.

By the end of the session Artemis was quite impressed. "You learn quickly, untitled one. You may leave now, and find your way home with Desdemona." She put a little emphasis on the name, then shuddered.

Zara was confused. "Where will I go, though?"

Artemis smiled, and retreated back into the shadows of the trees. "In the golden clouds of the Gods, you will always find your home."

Zara made her way out of the forest, Desdemona trotting behind her.

"My home... Maybe you can help me find it, Dem."

Desdemona immediately leapt ahead, sniffing at the silver paths and bridges, and running off in different directions. Zara hurried to follow, and nearly tripped when Desdemona stopped short at one of the bridges.

At the other end of the bridge sat another God, only he looked much younger and more careless than the ones Zara had seen earlier. He was looking up at the sun above him, and a chariot of gold lay behind him. From him came the feeling of heat and warmth. His sandy blonde hair was ragged, and his face was calm and emotionless. Zara watched in awe as he opened his eyes and looked from her to Desdemona.

"I see you have met my sister, Godling. You have already taken one of her wolves as your partner." His mouth stretched into an amused smile.

Zara tried to find her voice, and found that she did not have one. Desdemona growled disapproval and flicked her head.

"Speechless. Always speechless, aren't they? It's hard to make conversation with anyone anymore. Is it because of my newfound bad reputation? Or perhaps because I look frightening just sitting there, taken for unconscious." The man sighed. "My name is Apollo, and I am twin to Artemis. I am God of the Sun, and the Prophecy."

Zara snapped out of her trance. "You don't look anything like Artemis. Artemis is Goddess of the

Moon, the Hunt, and Feminine Life. How can you two be twins?"

Apollo looked offended. "I don't have to look like Artemis to be her twin. We are opposites of each other. She owns the Moon, I own the Sun. And I ride its symbol as proof." Apollo motioned towards the golden chariot behind him, which glowed.

Zara nodded, understanding. "Um, I was wondering whether I could go past you."

Apollo's bright face darkened. "Oh no, you don't. You aren't going down onto Earth. That's what I'm guarding. I was told to by Zeus."

Desdemona barked aggressively. Zara took a step forward. "I need to pass. Desdemona says it leads to home. Move aside."

Apollo heaved himself up. "Uh, sorry, you'll have to beat me in a fight to do that, little one. And since you just challenged me, you have to fight me now. No backing out or running away. I'll always catch you."

Zara took out her bow and slid an arrow in. "Bring it on."

Apollo laughed. "First one to fall. If you think those arrows are about to pierce my skin, you obviously do not know of my speed."

Then he lunged forwards, and Zara dodged swiftly, firing an arrow at his neck first. His hand shot up where the arrow had struck, and he plucked it out, a trickle of gold leaking out. He leaned down to look at her.

"You actually shot me," he growled menacingly. He tossed the arrow to the ground. "Not even Artemis can do that first shot."

Zara ducked as he aimed a blow at her head, and shot another three arrows up one leg, and again on the other side. He yelled in surprise and tripped, falling flat on his face.

Zara stood over him. "You said first to fall. Therefore, I win."

Apollo got up, his face like thunder. "You cheated..."

Zara frowned. "I got you fair and square. You tripped. You fell. You were first to. I can pass."

Apollo tried to stop her, but found he was tied to the spot. The arrows stuck in his shins bled gold. "I... am tied by the prophecy. First to fall."

Zara nodded and walked past, over to the chariot. She touched it and brought away her fingertip, seared and scorched red. Then she looked beyond, and a yawning hole stared back at her.

"Is that the only way down?" Zara asked, her voice trembling slightly.

"Unless you want to barbecue yourself on my chariot, you have to jump down and think of where you want to go or who you want to see," Apollo replied, pulling the arrows from his legs. Instantly, the wounds healed over.

Zara bit her lip, and looked at Desdemona. "Is this really the way?"

Desdemona nodded her black head, then jumped into the hole and disappeared. Zara looked back at Apollo, then jumped down with her, and pictured Hades in her mind.

When she opened her eyes, all she saw was black. After a while her eyes adjusted, and she saw the glimmer of white in the corners of the room. Bones, she realised. Human bones.

A large, gleaming red throne was centred in the room. It was facing away from her and she could see the pale hands of Hades wrapped over the sides. His helmet sat next to the throne, and in the distance she could hear strangled cries.

She walked towards the throne cautiously. "Hades? Is that you?"

"WHO HAS FOLLOWED ME INTO MY REALM?! WHO HAS DARED APPROACH ME, SAID MY NAME ALOUD AND SNEAKED UP BEHIND ME?!" Hades roared and his voice echoed around the room.

Zara winced, and looked over at Desdemona, who had reappeared at her side. "I am sorry, Lord Hades, Desdemona led me here."

Hades' throne spun around, and Zara looked up at him. He was no different than before, except this time he had rings of steel chaining him to the throne.

"You name your dog Desdemona. Why?" Hades asked.

Zara stood straighter, and Desdemona whined slightly. "Her eyes. They told me what she wanted to be called."

Hades shook his head. "I sent her to bring you here. She told you what her name was. She actually despises her name. Desdemona, here, you can transform back now."

Desdemona leapt over to Hades' side. Once she got there, her whole figure changed, rippled, melted and reformed, until a ghastly winged woman, glowing red, stood beside Hades.

"A fury. One of the three I control. You have done well, Desdemona. Now I dismiss you back to your realm," Hades said, waving his hand passively.

Desdemona shimmered and disappeared, crying out for a reward. Zara felt the blood drain from her face as Hades turned back to her.

"Now, Zara, will you be my apprentice?" Hades asked, his fingers rapping on the black stone of his throne.

Zara hesitated. "That wasn't why I came."

Hades leant forward. "But you can free me. If I have an apprentice, I am free to wander. Only by chance did

Ares summon me out of my cruel domain. But you, you can help me."

Zara shook her head. "But that's not what I came for."

Hades now looked angered. "Then leave. If you come back again and refuse my offer, I will make sure you don't find what you came for."

Zara took a step forward. "I must pass. Desdemona said my home was beyond here."

Hades tried to stand up, but his shackles held him back. "You may not pass."

Zara looked at him with pity. "I know this is a bad situation for you, but nobody gets what they want all the time. I did not get Desdemona as the lifelong friend I thought she would be. But I need my home. This is yours. Mine is beyond."

Hades eyes blazed. "This is not my home!" he shouted, trying to get up.

Zara walked past him and his stone throne. "Perhaps it is not, but for now, it is all you have." And she broke into a run, into the beyond.

There was nothing but blackness, but somehow Zara knew the way. She met no one, and no one came out to challenge her. She felt her feet stop short and she tipped forwards, shock registering on her face.

A steep hill crumbled down a cliff face to a beach. She could see the outline of a small beach house beyond the sand, floating on the water. Gravel-like rocks tumbled over the cliff face she was standing over. Even though she truly tried to deny it, she felt that this was home.

Zara leant over the cliff. "Uh, hello? Does anybody have a ladder?"

There was no reply, except for her echo repeating back at her. Zara prepared herself to jump, and was about to when a hand clamped down on her shoulder, and held her firmly. She tried to wrench the hard fingers off her shoulder, but they would not budge. Zara turned slowly, afraid of what she might see.

And she saw another Goddess, who was beautiful beyond imagining. Her eyes twinkled jade and her face was like her own: sharp and serious. Her teeth were perfectly straight, and all small. She wore a dress of hot pink, and her feet were laced in Greek sandals with wings on them. Her hair was tied back with a bobby pin that had a heart decoration on it.

"My dear, I think it is time to leave now. You don't want to go down there. Here, come with me back to the golden clouds of our realm," she said, her voice dazzlingly sweet and sugary.

"Who are you?" Zara asked, although she thought she already knew.

"Aphrodite, Goddess of Love and Beauty, my dear. Come, come, we must leave now if we are to make it," Aphrodite said, her voice breaking a little to reveal worry.

Zara nodded and followed Aphrodite back through the darkness. Soon they were back in Hades' chamber, where he was shouting insults at Aphrodite.

"You think you are beautiful, Aphrodite, but really, you aren't. All you've done is make yourself a pretty shell and walked inside it, hiding what you really are," Hades snarled as Zara was dragged along to the back of the room.

"Oh, shut it, Hades. You speak such gibberish sometimes," Aphrodite sighed.

Hades would not shut it. "Freedom of speech down here, Aphrodite. I can say whatever I like. Your real face must be twisted, Aphrodite, because right now, your aura sure is."

Aphrodite turned to him, gripping Zara's hand. "I grant your permission to leave this horrid realm, Zara, whilst I make Hades' life miserable just by standing here."

Zara felt herself being transported back to the golden clouds in a breeze of silver. She found herself standing on the paving just before the black hole. Apollo was back on guard, and he didn't look like he was about to let her pass again, either.

"I demand a rematch," Apollo growled when he saw Zara. He was now holding a glowing sword that shimmered with flames. Zara eyed it warily.

"Okay then! Try not to fall over this time," Zara jeered, ducking as Apollo thrust his sword forwards.

She felt at her back for her arrows, bow, and quiver, but realised with surprise that they were gone. She rolled between Apollo's legs as he brought down his sword again, and latched onto one of them. She had no weapon but strategy, it seemed.

Apollo roared as she bit into his leg and started stumbling backwards. Zara felt a surge of panic that he would fall on top of her, squashing her flat. Quickly, she let go and rolled aside as he fell down.

Apollo got up again immediately. "You will pay, you untitled one! I demand a match until one of us is so wounded we cannot go on, and you don't have a choice whether you will fight or not!"

Zara got up warily. As Apollo lifted his sword to strike, she stood firmly and raised her hand. The sword came crashing down, and Zara closed her eyes, preparing for the worst.

The sound of steel ringing against steel filled her ears, and she opened her eyes. The sword had come down, all right, but had landed on her palm, and not sliced through. Apollo stared in surprise at the sword and her hand, too shocked to do anything. But why had the sword stayed, and not sliced through? Zara did not know.

Zara clung to the sword, pulling it down. It came to rest at her feet, and she put her foot on it.

"I do not want to fight, Apollo. You are a sore loser. Think about that while I'm gone, for it is your one true weakness," Zara said, taking her foot off the sword. Then she walked away, with Apollo still staring at the sword.

Artemis was standing at the edge of the bridge. She looked astounded. "You beat my brother in battle. You held back a sword that was taller than you, and brought it to your feet with your bare hands," she smiled suddenly, her face revealing hope. "I think you are ready to see Zeus now."

Zara frowned. "He said by the end of this week."

Artemis laughed. "Oh, that is far too long for you. Right here, right now, is when you will see Zeus. Let us go to him."

CHAPTER FOUR

Ready or Not?

Zara felt slightly smaller as she walked up the spiral staircase a second time, Artemis behind her and Astra at her heels. The stairs were much longer, and by the time she reached the top, her face was deathly pale and her breaths came short and shallow.

Artemis looked over her, concerned. "Are you feeling all right, my archer?"

Zara shook her head desperately. "No. I... I think I'm nervous. Really nervous."

Artemis patted her back confidently. "Don't you worry; Zeus has a clear eye. He will love your efforts. Now go forth and shout his name. He will appear for you."

Zara stumbled forwards, tripping over herself. Her arrows rattled around in her new quiver; Artemis had replaced the old leather one with a new silver-woven one with shining stars and moons. "A symbol of honour, untitled one; it is one of my greatest creations. Treat it well," Artemis had said.

Now it seemed heavy against her back, and weighed her down. She could hear the fading footsteps of Artemis leaving down the stairs, and the padding sounds of Astra trotting down beside her.

"Zeus!" Zara tried to cry out, but only a strangled moan escaped her throat. She tried again, summoning her confidence. "Zeus! Hear me and come!"

A crackle of electricity erupted above her head. What looked like lightning struck the ground before her, and Zeus appeared out of nowhere.

"The untitled one returns. Come to me, and tell me why you are here."

Zara cleared her throat. "I have come from the training of Lady Artemis, and present myself to show my skills."

Zeus shook his head. "After one day? Impossible. Hercules needed more training than that."

"Artemis believes I am ready, therefore I am," Zara declared stubbornly, folding her arms.

Zeus turned his back on her. "Leave me. Your arrogance annoys me. Tell Artemis to get a brain."

Zara felt anger rise inside of her. She pulled an arrow from her quiver and placed it in her bow, aiming carefully at the centre of Zeus's skull. Then the arrow let fly, and Zeus shouted out.

The arrow had struck its target better than Zara had expected. Zeus fell forwards onto his face, unconscious. Zara lowered her bow and raised her head triumphantly.

"Artemis already has a brain. Unfortunately, now you have brain damage," Zara muttered, turning on her heel and running down the stairs.

She found Artemis awaiting her at the bottom. "That was quick."

Zara nodded. "I made it quick."

Artemis's eyes widened in sudden understanding. "You shot him?! You actually dared shoot Zeus?!"

Zara nodded again, this time a little anxiously. "He was being insulting towards you."

But Artemis was not unhappy. In fact, she was thrilled. "I will call Poseidon. You, go up and guard Zeus. Make sure he doesn't wake up. And take his Master Bolt."

Zara raised an eyebrow. "Why?"

"I wish Poseidon to take the throne. Poseidon will be a better ruler than Zeus," Artemis explained, glee lighting her face.

"What is so bad about Zeus?" Zara asked.

Artemis frowned. "Zeus is unjust, and punishes people for no reason. He set my brother to guard the Hole for simply riding his chariot whilst Zeus planned a storm. Apollo is now exhausted. That is why he fought so lousily against you."

That brought another question to Zara's mind. "Why was I able to stop his sword? How could I do that with my hands alone?"

Artemis went quiet. "I... I think your title is being revealed. I cannot understand it all yet, but some bits are clear."

Zara nodded, a little disappointed, but all the same, that was all Artemis could tell her. She bounded up the stairs and found Zeus lying where he had been before. But now puddles of liquid gold covered the floor around his body, and the wound in the back of his head had closed over, with the arrow still sticking out.

Zara picked up the Master Bolt beside Zeus and held it up. Her hair sprang into ringlets as jolts of electricity flew through her veins. She felt herself growing upwards further and further, until she was at the height of Zeus himself. Sparks of electric blue danced along her fingertips. Zara looked down at the floor in amazement, bewildered by the fact she had grown so quickly.

Zeus didn't look like he was about to get up again very soon. Some of his fingers twitched, and his eyes fluttered momentarily, but apart from that, he was as still as a statue.

Zara turned her head sharply when she heard the noise of distant footsteps hurrying up the stairs. Artemis and Poseidon came into view at the top of the stairwell, and both looked shocked to see Zara standing there, as tall as them both, and holding the Bolt in her hand.

Artemis finally managed a smile. "Congratulations, Zara. You are now a true Goddess while you hold the Bolt in your hand. Now, open the door to your right so we can go in. The Master Bolt should do the trick on the lock."

Zara looked over to her right, to the door that Zeus had first come through. A small engraving of a crown was upon it. There was no doorknob, only a simple round keyhole the size of the Bolt's tip in the middle of the crown. Zara walked over and poked the Bolt in and turned it like a handle.

The door swung open. Poseidon, who had not said a word, rushed forwards and inside before Zara could take a peek. Artemis followed quickly, and gestured for Zara to follow.

Zara tiptoed into the grand room. The walls were not made of stone, but large transparent electric fields, and you could see beyond them over the clouds. There was a large, bright blue throne at the end of the room, which Poseidon had already seated himself upon. He looked victorious, and Zara saw water rising from the ground to create his Crystal Trident in his hand. Artemis knelt before him, her face full of glee. She was holding a crescent moon in her hand.

Zara walked over. "What is the point of this? To know your brother will be annoyed if you sit upon his throne? To mess around with his belongings, and make him angered?" she said, irritated by the look of childish triumph on Poseidon's face.

Poseidon's face turned serious. "These will be my things soon. I must await Artemis. She is remembering the crowning lines. I must give her time."

"So all you want is your brother's things?" Zara asked, pulling a face. The statues in the room were all of Zeus himself, in a pose of glory or power. Did Poseidon really wish to own those things?

Poseidon shook his head and laughed. "You will see, child. Artemis, are you ready? I am impatient to be King of the Gods."

Artemis nodded hurriedly. Then she began to speak ancient Greek. Zara couldn't understand anything except the fact it was ceremonial, and a speech. When Artemis finished, Poseidon lifted his head and stamped his Trident on the ground. The statues in the room changed to statues of Poseidon holding his Crystal Trident in similar poses to the ones the Zeus statues had been in.

Zara looked around, stupefied. "So that's what you wanted? Statues of yourself? Gosh, statues must be rare around here if you're so incredibly desperate for them."

Poseidon frowned in irritation. "Child, I have just thrown Zeus off his high horse and now I am King of the Gods. All the Gods and Goddesses will do as I command from now on. Even my brother, Zeus. And if he does not obey, he will meet our father in Tartarus."

Zara nodded slowly. "Why did you need to do that, though?"

Artemis cut in. "Zeus's rule was unjust. I told you that before. That reminds me, Poseidon. Our deal? Is Apollo now freed?"

Poseidon smiled at Artemis. "I hereby relieve Apollo of his duty to guard the Hole. He may now continue on his way."

Artemis smiled widely. "Thank you. I must leave now, to welcome him back. I promised him a round of hunting."

And she left, running down the stairs with her bow in her hand.

Poseidon now turned to Zara, who stood rigid.

"I must reward you for your service to me, Zara. What do you want? Something pretty, for someone your age? Or something that shows your obedient personality. What would you like?" Poseidon asked.

Zara jumped at this opportunity. She thought of all the things she had ever wanted. Next she thought of the other Gods and Goddesses. What would they like? Then the idea came to her. It was a large request, but a worthy one.

"I wish to have Hades freed," Zara said loudly, and in a stately way. She wanted Poseidon to know she was serious.

Poseidon raised an eyebrow and leant back in the throne, which was now a calming blue, and had bubbles of foam on the edges. "That is a very hard request to grant. You know that, don't you?"

Zara nodded. "But it is fair. He wants nothing more than to leave and explore. He has been tortured, living with the dead, hearing their stories day after day. He wants to be in the presence of the living. He wants to live up here, with us."

Poseidon frowned. "Who will take care of the Underworld, though? We cannot let it run wild. The dead may have plans of their own to wage war. Only Hades stands in the way of that happening."

Zara thought about it. "The Fates will take care of them. They create death for a reason, so people can have the rest to match what their life was worth. Sleeping is not enough. The dead do not want war, but peace. Hades drives them mad by yelling at them all day. They want him out too."

Poseidon leant forward. "You understand the dead very well, child. Why is that?"

Zara lifted her head. "Another of my powers is the ability to understand, I think. It seems you do not possess that power, since you need my explanations."

"Do not be arrogant. You may hold the Master Bolt, but my Crystal Trident now symbolises the powers of a God. That Bolt is merely a weapon now," Poseidon warned.

"My request. Do you have an answer?" Zara asked, growing impatient.

Poseidon ran his fingers under his chin. "I will grant your request on one condition."

Zara rolled her eyes. "There's always a catch."

"The condition is you must figure out how to free him. I have no knowledge of how he is tied to that spot in the Underworld. Zeus secretly banished him under our noses when Hades found the Helm of Shadows. Now go forth and undo my brother's wrong." Poseidon waved his hand dismissively.

Zara balled her hands into fists. "I know how to free him already. But I don't want to do it."

Poseidon shook his head and laughed. "You must sacrifice some things to get what you want, child."

Zara placed down the Bolt, shrinking in size as she did so. "I must become his apprentice to free him. That I do not want to do."

"What does he have to teach you? You already know everything he does. If you become his apprentice, all you have to do is go on a quest every now and then for him. If you do, you will be free. Sound all right to you?" Poseidon explained, smiling.

Zara nodded doubtfully. "I'll go now. You deal with the Bolt." She turned on her heel quickly, trying to hide the disbelief in her voice. She then left the room, the electricity from the Master Bolt still crackling and sparking through her hair.

The door slammed behind her. Zara turned to look, and saw the keyhole had changed. Three holes went through the door, a distance of around twenty centimetres between each one. Zara remembered that was how the Trident had been crafted. It was strange how the power had shifted so easily.

"Where is my Bolt? Get me my Bolt!" a voice growled behind her. Zara jumped around to see Zeus getting up into a kneeling position. The arrow was now in his hand.

Zara froze. "Uh, you might want to look through those keyholes there. You no longer rule over the Gods."

Zeus stood up. He was as tall as any normal man now. "Liar. You wouldn't know anything about that. Now, have you touched my Bolt? Your hair gives you away, its power is leaping around you. Hand it over."

Zara shook her head. "I no longer possess it. Poseidon, King of the Gods, now holds it."

Zeus pushed Zara aside and banged on the door with the three holes. It swung open, and Zeus cried out in anguish. He ran forwards and fell to his knees. Zara strained to look past into the room, and was not surprised by what she saw.

Poseidon had skewered the Master Bolt with the tips of the Crystal Trident. It fizzed with electricity being snuffed out in the presence of water. Poseidon leered over Zeus jeeringly. "Your precious treasure is destroyed, Zeus. You are powerless. You are under my command. Look around at what you have lost. I now own everything of yours."

Zara thought she saw a tear trickle down Zeus's face. "You do not know what you have done. All Hades will break loose. He will not enjoy this."

"Oh, he will. He is going to be freed by Zara over there. She knows how to. Zara, why don't you go do that now?" Poseidon asked, suddenly noticing her standing in the doorway.

Zara nodded stiffly. She turned and left Poseidon to taunt his brother. She thought of it as cruel. Although Zeus had done many wrongs, his last possession should not have been destroyed. Perhaps taken for a while from him, but not destroyed.

The walk down the stairs was agonizingly long. Zara wondered whether it was her own speed that was doing this, or whether they had increased in length because of Poseidon's wish. When she reached the bottom she collapsed to her knees, and found it hard to even take in shaky breaths. Everything was exhausting her. Was it always like this for Gods and Goddesses, or was it just her?

Struggling to get up, Zara saw a crowd of Gods and Goddesses at the door. They were trying to get in, and were beating on the glass of the double doors. Or what looked like glass. It was actually a shield of water, thick and transparent. Zara rushed over to open it for them, but was restrained by her own tiredness. Slowly, she slipped out of consciousness and slumped to the floor.

CHAPTER FIVE

Friend and Foe

Zara woke up with blurry vision, and the feeling of freezing cold against her forehead. She raised her head slowly and rubbed her eyes gently to remove the thick layer of water that was blinding her. A throbbing pain pulsed through her fingers and every now and then she felt a jolt of electricity leave her. It was hard to tolerate.

"Up and rise. Up and rise. Come on, Godling, you have had your beauty sleep. Up and rise. Up and rise," a gruff, throaty voice growled from nearby.

Zara blinked thoroughly and finally saw the world with clear vision. A man with a short, roughly-cropped beard and tangled, thick brown hair running down over his shoulders sat before her. His face, mellow and friendly, was covered in wrinkles, and his skin was worn and dusty brown. His eyebrows were knitted together in concern. He wore leather armour and had a large battle axe slung over his shoulder. A scar showed under his left eye, and the musky brown of his irises was darkened by worry.

Zara sat up properly and propped her head back against the bed frame. "Who are you?"

The man gave a short grunt. "Of course, I forgot you hadn't met us all. I am Hephaestus, God of the Forge. I create weapons for the Gods and Goddesses."

"Did you make the Master Bolt and the Crystal Trident?" Zara asked, as she saw them as powerful weapons.

Hephaestus shook his head. "No, no. Those were forged by the Earth, or if you call her by her real name, Gaea. I am but a crippled creator of sturdy weapons made of steel and other strong metals. I do not mess with magic, as Earth did to make those weapons. Gaea made a mistake with those. A grave mistake."

Zara looked around. She was sitting up in a simple wooden bed, and around her was a small room with stools, tables and tools, and a fireplace for forging weapons. The man before her held a pair of strong, metal tongs and in between the pincers was a bag of ice, which was quickly melting in the heat of the room, with water dripping off it onto the ground, sizzling and evaporating.

"If you've got the strength now, hop up and put your feet in the ice slippers. Not exactly high standard glass, but that would melt here. Those slippers are enchanted not to melt, so just make sure you wear them, or have your feet burned. Your choice," Hephaestus grumbled, getting up and walking over to the forging table, where he lay down the ice pack and picked another from a small, seemingly enchanted electric freezer. Seeing Zara staring at it in surprise, he shrugged his shoulders. "I couldn't find anything else that would keep the ice cold and be enchanted into not melting itself at the same time." He explained. He then slammed the lid closed and trudged over to Zara again, holding the ice pack in the tongs carelessly.

Zara slung her feet over the side and slipped her feet into the icy shoes on the ground. They felt cool against her skin, but other than that, they felt silky like the slippers she used to wear when she lived with Ares.

Zara frowned at the thought. She despised Ares now for the unjust way he had imprisoned her without speaking of it to Zeus. But, Zara thought, would Zeus have cared? Most likely not, according to what Artemis had said.

Hephaestus waved the tongs and ice pack around impatiently. "Come on then, Godling, I have to get back to work."

Zara stood up and crossed her arms. "Don't be such a pill. You can tolerate me for a while more, I'm sure.

You probably already have plenty of armour, shields, weapons and the rest of your handiwork."

Hephaestus straightened up proudly. "I make over one thousand swords a day, Godling, so watch your manners."

"Watch yours. So, if you're the God who crafts the weapons, do you lead them into battle? By the size of the battle axe upon your back, I'd say so," Zara observed.

Hephaestus's eyes burned with fury at the mention of war. "You think I would lead a war?! Godling, you have much to learn. War is the thing I hate most. The Gods are always having their fights with the Titans. It is annoying to see how often they childishly come back to tease their elders. Peace and a little respect wouldn't go astray with this odd bunch. I stand back whilst they rage their wars. I only want peace."

"Then why do you make them weapons for it?" Zara asked, pointing at a pile of daggers and swords heaped over by the burning coals.

Hephaestus followed her finger to where she was pointing. "Ah, those. I do not give those to the Gods, but to my worthy apprentices down on Earth. They run my errands for me."

Zara frowned. "Why do you need people to do your duties for you? You look strong enough."

Hephaestus's eyes softened sadly. "I am crippled, Godling. See my legs? They are bruised and battered, and the bones are worn out and being ground to dust even as I walk. I cannot fight, Godling. I am far too weak."

Zara looked down at Hephaestus's legs. She hadn't noticed before, but they were purple, black and blue, and very wizened. "Who did that to you? Surely it didn't come with age."

Hephaestus looked up at the roof and fiddled with the tongs. The ice had already melted. "My mother, Hera, Goddess of Heaven, threw me off a cliff when I was born. As you can see, I am quite ugly, and the only God to be like that. She was appalled by my lack of handsomeness, and despised me, even though I was her own child. I have been like this from childbirth, Godling, and forever I will be."

Zara looked him up and down pityingly. "You aren't ugly. Perhaps you aren't as grand as Zeus, as young-looking as Hades or as welcoming as Poseidon, but you are probably the wisest of the three of them put together. I can see by your face you have seen many things, and not all were good. You have wisdom, and perhaps that was all you ever needed to get through your life."

Zara jumped as a bang at the door rattled it against its hinges. "Let me in! I must speak with the Godling! She has insulted me."

Hephaestus sighed. "Coming, Athena. But please, do not be too harsh. She has not even met you yet, and she has little knowledge of you."

He limped over to the door slowly. When he opened it, a woman with bright orange, long straight hair burst inside in full Greek armour, aiming a spear at Zara's heart.

Zara raised a hand and waggled her fingers, carefully placing her other hand over her heart for protection. "Hi. Another Goddess I don't know. What's your title?"

The woman with orange hair raised herself up placidly and put her nose in the air. "I am Athena, Goddess of Wisdom and Battle Strategy. And I believe you said Hephaestus was wiser than the three top Gods put together. Which is untrue. The old fool doesn't even know his history."

Hephaestus growled behind her, baring his teeth in anger. Athena ignored him, and went on.

"That is an insult to my wisdom. Take it back now, or I will drive my spear through your heart," Athena snarled.

Zara dropped her 'hello' hand but kept the other over her heart. "I won't take it back. Perhaps he is wiser than those three, but I never said he was wiser than you."

Athena gritted her teeth. "Find yourself in Tartarus when you awaken, Godling."

With a lightning thrust, she sent the spear flying. Zara zipped forwards and wrapped her arms around the spear before it had even got close. She hastily brought it down on her knee, cracking it in two. She shoved the point into her quiver in a smooth, fast movement to hide what she had taken.

Athena gasped and went bright red. "My spear! You–"

Zara held the end of it in her hand. "You showed neither wisdom nor battle strategy when you tried to kill me. You were predictable. I could see what you would do from the start."

Athena lifted her chin. "I was blinded by anger."

Zara smiled jeeringly. "You are not a good liar, Athena. To make excuses is to be cowardly and not face the facts. Maybe your title is wrong."

Athena stormed out of the forge looked thunderous. Hephaestus winced as he limped over to Zara. "You've made an enemy out of Athena. Congratulations, you're the first to want to be on her bad side."

Zara suddenly remembered Hades down in the underworld. "I have to go now. Thank you for your hospitality," and she bolted out the door, stopping just as she left to slip on her boots that were waiting by the doormat.

Zara found the Hole much more easily this time as Apollo wasn't hiding it with the sun chariot. Speedily, she slipped down and in and thought of Hades' face.

The blackness enveloped Zara again, and she blinked ten times hurriedly to get on with it. Once Hades' throne came into view, she leapt up and strode over to it. Just before she reached it, the throne spun around and Hades began to yell.

"GET OUT!" he roared, his red eyes flashing.

Zara didn't hesitate. She clamped her hand over his mouth and started fiddling with the lock of the shackles that tied him to the throne.

"I'm helping you, numbskull. I'm your apprentice. I'm letting you free."

Zara felt a sharp pain in the hand over Hades' mouth and brought it away quickly. Bite marks punctured it and already something black was spreading beneath her skin and inner veins.

"Why? Why didn't you just agree in the first place? Why did you leave me here with... with Aphrodite and make me moody for the rest of the day?" Hades shouted angrily.

Zara finally found the spring and pulled the shackles off Hades' hands. "Let's go."

Hades stayed put. "Answer me!"

Zara turned and glared at him. "I had to go home." Then she turned and walked back over to where she had come from. "Do you want to be free, or not?"

Hades leapt up and followed, looking slightly interested. "Where are you taking me?"

Zara smiled slyly. "To the home of the Gods. Where you actually belong. Now," she paused, trying to remember what Aphrodite had said to let her go free, back to the clouds, "I grant you permission to leave this horrid realm, Hades. Watch yourself, for Poseidon now rules."

Zara felt herself being twisted back into the silvery mass of air, and closed her eyes.

CHAPTER SIX

Dead or Alive?

The clouds were there again, but they were not gold anymore. They were a rich transparent blue, and the bridges were made of sand and seashells. Already, it seemed, Poseidon was taking a hand to renovating the city atop the clouds.

The great tower had changed too. Instead of the gold, it was made entirely of sand. Gigantic shells opened as windows and intricate patterns were engraved in the double doors, now foaming with bubbles at the handles.

"So this is what Olympus really looks like," Hades murmured from beside Zara, looking over the clouds admiringly.

Zara nodded. "This is all new. Poseidon wished to change things, and their looks, it seems. Come, we must speak with him."

Zara walked over bridges with Hades following close behind. She realised that he was at a normal height now, not the giant of a man he had been before. When had that happened? When she actually thought about it, neither had Hephaestus been abnormally tall either. Was this another of Poseidon's changes?

Zara pushed open the double doors easily. They were lighter than the thick gold ones had been when Zeus had sat upon the throne. Zara wondered what was happening to Zeus right now. Was he safe, or was he being jeered at by Poseidon? The very thought made Zara frown in irritation.

The long spiral staircase had disappeared. In its place floated a glass lift suspended in mid-air. A glowing button labelled 'up' hovered just beneath it. Zara pushed it warily and the lift doors opened. Hades quickly stepped inside behind her, his face full of curiosity.

The lift went up faster than Zara had expected. She gripped the railing on the sides to reassure herself of her safety. She had never been one for heights.

Hades, beside her, looked as though he felt the same way. His face was deathly pale and his hands gripped the railing until his knuckles turned white. He glanced sideways at Zara and grimaced.

"I've never been transported like this before. Really, a God shouldn't feel nauseous just being lifted upwards but, for some reason, I am faring badly."

Zara smiled half-heartedly. The lift came to a shuddering halt and the doors opened to reveal the large domed room. The door with the three pinholes was half open already, and from the other side came shouting voices. Zara and Hades stepped out of the lift cautiously and into the throne room.

Artemis was standing beside Apollo, who was stony-faced and cold. Artemis looked distraught. "I don't understand, Poseidon! Why do I have to go down to Earth on an expedition?! Apollo just got freed from his duty. Please. One more day?"

Poseidon shook his head solemnly. "No, Artemis. This is very important. The people of Earth must know that Zeus, God of the Sky, is dead."

Zara's eyes widened in astonishment and horror. Zeus was dead? How was that possible? Zeus had plenty left to live for. Had he really lost all hope?

Poseidon sighed and looked down at the ground, his hands folded in his lap. "I cannot change this turn of events that has so devastated our community. But the beings of Earth must know too. They praised him as their major God. They must be given the news."

Artemis folded her arms. "And you suppose, by this 'turn of events', they'll bow down to you straight away? Oh no, they will take it that you killed Zeus, and rebel against you. They will not worship you wholeheartedly. They will rage war against you, Poseidon. And human wars are not pretty."

Apollo now spoke up. "I believe the people must know, too. But this trip will take a long time. Up to a month. What if the people turn on Artemis? What if they don't believe her? See the possibilities, Poseidon, for they are endless. And I have had a prophecy come to me for The Oracle. I may not speak it aloud, but it ends gravely for my sister. However, it is in riddle form, so I know little."

Poseidon's eye caught sight of Zara in the doorway, her mouth still hanging open.

"Leave us now, Artemis and Apollo. I have new visitors."

Apollo and Artemis turned to see who it was. When Artemis saw Zara, she smiled sadly and looked down at the ground. However, when Apollo saw her he unsheathed his sword and yelled angrily, charging at her full speed. Zara merely raised a hand over her heart and the sword rebounded off it, and Apollo flew backwards.

Poseidon's eyes widened at this. "Go now, Apollo. Your eagerness for revenge displeases me. And Artemis, go down and tell them the news. No more defiance, reasoning or negotiation. Go!"

Artemis hurried out of the room and Apollo brushed past Zara, giving her the evil eye. Zara took a few steps into the room, shuddered, and retreated back to the door.

"What is wrong, child? What bothers you?" Poseidon asked, his face filled with concern.

"Zeus didn't die because he lost all he stood for. He still has things to stand for. He still rules the sky. His Bolt may be gone, but all it did was symbolise power. He didn't fade away. If anything, he's most likely still alive, but being bent to do your will," Zara said slowly, rubbing her head. A surge of cold had overtaken her when she had gone forwards. "Or, if he really is dead, you killed him."

Poseidon stood at this accusation. He was as tall as any normal man now. "Me? Kill my brother? Are you going insane, child?"

Zara shook her head, clearing her mind. "Can we move on, Poseidon? I am not feeling well."

Poseidon sat down, still looking a little outraged. "Okay. Where is Hades? Did you succeed, or did he try to burn you to ashes and use them to decorate his grim country?"

Hades stepped forward from behind the doorframe. "My country is not grim, just mistaken. And I would never try to burn Zara here. She is my apprentice now."

Zara moved forwards again, going slowly so as to be able to dodge the spot where it was cold. There was a slight shadow on the ground where she had stood before. Zara eyed it curiously, whilst still carefully approaching Poseidon.

Hades followed, but went through the cold spot. Immediately, he shouted and his eyes blazed. He stepped back and held his head, his face twisted in agony.

Poseidon got up and strode over to Hades. "Are you all right, brother?"

Hades was still holding his head, but his face was calming now. "A ghoul spot. I need my Helm of Shadows but I forgot to bring it."

Zara thought of the Helm, with its delicate Greek engravings and black sheen. It did seem like it would make you into shadows, simply by looking at it.

A slight noise of rushing air sounded behind Zara, and something banged into her back, knocking her over. Zara caught herself just before she landed face first on the marble floor. She heard Poseidon curse darkly and Hades mutter angrily. Wondering what had hit her, she got up and turned around.

The Helm lay on the ground behind her. It looked darker and shinier than ever. Zara picked it up and turned it over in her hands, inspecting the Greek lettering. She could not read it, but she knew it spoke of evil and eternal darkness. How she had summoned it she was not sure, but she felt she had a strong connection to the helm, and its powers.

Before Hades or Poseidon could stop her, she lifted the Helm of Shadows to her head and slid it on.

Everything became darker immediately. Zara saw Poseidon and Hades searching around the room for her, avoiding the dark spot on the ground that Hades had called a ghoul spot.

But now atop the shadow over that spot was a spirit. A man, paler than sheets and transparent, hovered over it. His face was distraught and saddened, lined with grief. Zara instantly recognised who it was.

"Zeus! So you really are dead?" Zara whispered.

The spirit nodded. "I had no more to represent. My sky is now under Poseidon's rule. Poseidon destroyed my only means of power. I could never take the throne back without my weapon."

Zara rolled her eyes at the drama of it all. "Did you ever think to make a new weapon?"

The spirit paused. "No."

Zara threw up her hands in exasperation. "Then get a new one! You could easily take the throne back then."

Zeus now shook his head. "You don't understand. Once you die as a God, you can't simply reappear. I'm gone now. Tell Hera I'm sorry."

Zara made a face, disgusted. "You are so cliché."

And with that, Zeus disappeared from the shadowed spot, and the shadow itself disappeared too. Zara felt someone's hands clamp down on her shoulders, and pull her back. The Helm came off her head and rolled to the ground.

Zara winced at the sudden brightness of the world. Hades was holding onto her shoulders, and he looked really mad.

"How dare you wear my Helm, and run off with it! Is that all you wanted from being my apprentice? You will be severely punished for this, Godling," Hades hissed in her ear.

Poseidon picked up the helm. "Do not be harsh on her, Hades. She was reading the writing, which tells you to put it on and talk to the dead. It is a curse that she bore for a few minutes, Hades, but even then, how would you feel with the rage of the dead screaming and howling at you? Has she not suffered enough?"

Hades dropped his hands off Zara's shoulders, who instantly stepped forwards as a precaution. "Of course, you are right, Poseidon. No one is able to resist the Helm's curse but me. Only I am used to its power. Now, Godling," Hades said, turning to Zara, "what did you hear and see?"

"Zeus was standing over the ghoul spot. He told me that now that Poseidon rules his sky, he cannot take it back, his Bolt being destroyed and all," Zara said sullenly. She eyed Poseidon with a suspicious glance. "In some ways, Poseidon, you have murdered your brother."

Poseidon opened his mouth to speak, looking enraged. Hades silenced him with a wave of his hand. "If what Zara says is true, she is correct, and you will no longer rule the throne. That would leave the burden to me to rule over the Gods. Now, Poseidon, the girl must give us proof."

"He told me to tell Hera he was sorry, whoever she is. But I don't think he gave me any proof to show he spoke to me. I'm afraid you are only as much as a lawyer without a case," Zara said stiffly, still glaring at Poseidon suspiciously.

Poseidon crossed his arms and walked out of the room. As soon as he had left, Hades spun Zara around to face him. "Check your pockets."

Zara was confused. "What? Why?"

Hades tapped his foot impatiently. "Do it."

Zara shoved her hands in her pockets and found, in her right one, something cold and metallic. She pulled her hand out and put it to her eye, examining it closely.

Hades smiled. "We do have proof. A ghost coin. Keep it, they're quite valuable, and if you give it to a spirit they might serve you for a while."

Zara was now staring at the coin in horror. She tried to pull it off her finger, but it was stuck fast. Suddenly, her finger went a shiny pale blue and the coin sunk into and under her skin, melting inside. The finger went back to its normal colour, but now her fingernails were a sparkling, platinum blue.

Hades was watching, goggle-eyed. Zara looked up from her hand slowly.

"My hand just absorbed a ghost coin," she said dumbly.

Hades picked up his Helm of Shadows and started tapping it worriedly. "That should not have happened. No, this is unnatural."

Zara saw a speck of black on her wrist, and gasped. Her veins were filled with a black substance. She could see it from under the skin. Pulling up her sleeve, she saw it had spread along up her arm and had ended just below her shoulder.

"Hades. Remember when you bit me?" Zara frowned, her voice low and threatening.

Hades nodded, his brow furrowed in confusion. "Why do you ask of this now?"

Zara pulled up her sleeve again, displaying the black blood that was now rushing through her veins. "Well, is this another of your supernatural powers that's going to kill me?"

Hades eyes widened. "Oh, by Chaos, this is bad."

Zara nodded in agreement. "Yes, well duh."

Hades ran out of the room. "Stay there," he ordered, before getting into the elevator.

Zara frowned again. She wasn't about to obey orders from someone who had bitten her and given her some sort of disease. She walked out into the domed room and suddenly became curious about what the other doors held behind them. She pushed the one closest to her open, and went inside.

In this room were precious jewels – piles and mounds of gold and silver coins, incense sticks and other glimmering, sweet things. Zara picked up some of the gold coins, and, to her surprise, these also melded into her skin, which made her hand glow an unreal gold. Beneath a helmet something electric white gleamed, shining above all other things. Zara lifted the helmet and gasped.

The Master Bolt, broken into three, lay there, sparking and fizzing. Zara checked that no one was looking, and took the three pieces, shoving them into the pocket of her leather jacket, but resolved to find them somewhere safer when she found the chance. Zara slipped out of the room as quietly as she could.

The other door was already open a crack, but it was heavy and hard to push. After many rounds of trying to heave it away, it finally, with a grinding noise, slid backwards.

This room was empty of everything but a table piled with weapons. They were all made of some type of strong metal, and each had a valuable gem encrusted in the hilt. Zara rummaged through the pile, until she found a long, black-bladed dagger. It was lying under everything else, as if it wanted to be forgotten. After weighing it in her hands, she slid it into her belt and walked out of the room.

The lift had come back up again. It looked more un-safe and tilted than ever. She didn't want to go in there again. So instead she leapt over the railing around it, bracing herself for impact on the floor. She landed with excellent accuracy, and her arms and legs were not at all jarred from jumping from such a height.

Pushing open the double doors, she could just see Hades running over the bridges and to Ares' warplane. Quietly, she tiptoed over the bridges and into Artemis' forest.

It was denser than last time. The trees overhung more, and the leaves were dry and crinkled. Piles of leaves were scattered on the ground randomly. In the darker parts, Zara could see the flickers of yellow that Artemis had told her were wolves' eyes watching her every move.

Zara heard a small, saddened howl come from ahead. Speeding up, she found Astra, his eyes closed and a strong, heavy metal chain tying him to a tree.

"Hey, Astra. Did she leave you behind?" Zara called to Astra, who turned his great head towards her. His usually gold eyes were filled with tears, making them a dull yellow.

Zara scratched behind his ears. "Let's see whether I can break this chain for you, Astra."

Zara picked up the chain. It was quite heavy, and the metal was reinforced with something far stronger than ordinary iron. But again, the metal of the chain started to melt into her hand and disappeared under her skin in no time. Astra barked happily and tossed his head at the freedom of being able to move again.

Zara remembered the black veins, and pulled up her sleeve. The blackness was now well and truly past her shoulder, and seeping up her neck. She caught Astra looking at her curiously.

"Hades did this, Astra. Would you know of anything that would help?" Zara asked, rubbing his head.

Astra nodded and bounded off into the woods. He appeared again only seconds later, a crystal vial between his jaws. He dropped it before Zara and looked up at her expectantly,

Zara picked up the vial and read the label. "Ointment of Moondust. Use carefully. Do not eat."

Zara opened the lid cautiously. Inside the vial was a chalky dust. Zara poked her finger in and dabbed it on where the black blood had begun, over the bite marks. The black blood immediately disappeared and was replaced with silver that shot up her arm and into her neck. A coolness spread over Zara until the last hints of the black disease were gone.

Astra raised his head and howled at the sky. Zara smiled and twisted the lid back on the vial. "Thanks, Astra. Now, let's go. I've got something special for you to do."

Astra's brow furrowed in confusion and his golden eyes darkened. He barked deeply and bore his teeth.

"Come on, Astra. It's only little. I was wondering whether you could show me where Artemis lives. There's something in there I need."

Astra winced and whined in protest. Zara handed him the vial and crouched down at his height. "Astra, please. It's only a small thing."

Finally, Astra gave in and trotted through the woods with Zara close behind. He stopped before a large, hollowed oak with a still pool of water surrounding it. A tiny stone bridge led into a small hut inside the tree, with a roundish, egg-shaped door that was about a head shorter in height than Zara.

Astra looked over his shoulder at Zara and barked. Zara ducked down and went inside the hollow, careful to not touch anything that might be in her way. A large, hooded cloak with little silver strands with stars and moons dangling off the end hung upon a rack just in front of her. Zara snatched the cloak up and draped it over her shoulders.

She noticed a large pocket on the underside of the cloak, and took the Bolt pieces from her jacket, placing them into the cloak pocket. The thick folds of the cloak concealed the bump, and at last Zara felt the pieces were safe.

Astra whined from outside, and Zara hurried to the exit. Astra looked surprised to see the cloak over Zara, and started sniffing at the threads on the tail of the cloak. Zara moved silently on without touching Astra, and he watched her go.

"See you, Astra. And thank you. You have been a big help," Zara called quietly, disappearing into the trees.

Astra blinked a couple of times, then started sniffing at where Zara had disappeared. His ears were cocked back in utter confusion. After a while, he gave up, and trotted out of the forest.

CHAPTER SEVEN

Hero and Thief

Zara felt invisible in the cloak. But that felt great. Unseen. Nobody to stop her going where she wanted. That was what the cloak provided: the ability to blend into the sky.

She could see Poseidon and Hades arguing outside the sandy tower. Hades was probably wondering where she was, and Poseidon looked a little relieved that she had left, but he was trying to keep his face stern and worried.

Zara walked past them. Poseidon wasn't holding his Trident. That was good. She opened the door slightly and slipped inside. Poseidon and Hades didn't notice even when the door clicked shut.

She tiptoed up to the elevator. She disliked the fact she had to use it, but she had no choice other than to do so, so she pressed the button. It came down quickly.

Poseidon and Hades were still distracted in argument. Silently, the elevator lifted upwards gently, less violently than before.

In the throne room, Poseidon's Crystal Trident stood unattended. Zara slunk over and held the handle firmly. The power of water rushed through her; cool, refreshing, and strengthening. Unfortunately, somehow Poseidon had felt the power being unleashed too. She heard him roar in her mind and knew that he was storming over to the elevator.

Soon I will be with you, thief of unknown origin. And you will have nowhere to hide.

Zara snatched up the Trident and aimed it at the door. When Poseidon shoved it open, he saw three sharp points aimed at his heart, and tan fingers holding onto the hilt. A face shadowed by a hood was visible, but only a faint shimmer implied that it was actually a person standing before him.

"Hand me my Trident, unknown thief. Appear before me, and confess," Poseidon growled threateningly. Zara noticed how quickly his smiling eyes had changed to dark and murderous, and how fast his attitude had changed since he became ruler of the Gods.

Zara felt the cloak fighting off the spell of Poseidon, but it was weak. The hood started slipping off her head and back onto her neck. Quickly, Zara pulled it over her head tightly, and the cloak obeyed.

Hades appeared behind Poseidon, his face conveying suspicion. As his eyes gazed over Zara he blinked, as if surprised, then quickly stilled the expression and kept on searching.

His thoughts whispered in her mind. *I can see you, Goddess of Hiding. But I will not betray you. If you confess, Poseidon will reduce you to a pile of salt and coral, and I will be left for nothing back in the land of the dead. I cannot afford that. Slip away whilst I cause a distraction.*

Zara snorted in disapproval. *"So you're using me, for your own convenience?"* she thought back, a little surprised she'd managed it.

There was an angry growl on the other end of the thought-line. *You speak pretty confidently for one I could kill with a single snap of my fingers.*

Zara clutched the trident harder. *I'm confident that I'm going to win this fight. I'm going to escape from here. Just hold your breath, and you'll be fine.*

Wha–?

Zara's eyes flashed blue beneath her hood and she felt a surge of coolness rush over her, quickly replaced by a roaring in her ears and the feeling of salty waves crashing within her. She focused hard on the Trident, thinking of water and liquid, flowing, uncontrollable...

A wave of water burst from the end of the Trident, like a small tidal wave. Poseidon yelled and covered his eyes with his arms protectively. Hades only had time to gasp as the wave of water crashed down on him.

By the time all the water had flowed from the weapon, Poseidon lay soaking on the ground, spluttering and coughing. Hades let out his breath and streaks of salty water trailed down his face. He looked up at where Zara had been standing, but she had disappeared.

A whisper from behind him made him jump nervously. *Watch your belongings, my Lord.*

Hades turned around, and saw a shadowed face under a cloak. Only the mouth of the person was visible, and it was twitched into a mocking smile. Bright, shiny eyes glowed from the darkness of the hood.

Too late, Hades realised a tanned hand was reaching out from under the cloak. He felt it prise open his fingers from around his Helm, and it disappeared from under his grip. Hades grabbed out to get it back, but the cloaked figure shrank back and ran out of the room.

Poseidon got up, shaking his hands to dry off the water. "My Crystal Trident. That Goddess of Unknown took it, and got away with it!"

Hades turned to face Poseidon again. "I am afraid she took my Helm as well. I felt the presence of the Master Bolt, too, as she was in the room. She has all three weapons now."

Poseidon's fists clenched. "Then go after her! She is your apprentice, after all."

Hades pointed a finger at Poseidon. "Do your own dirty work in the future. I will have no part in it." He turned on his heel and left.

Just as he reached the elevator, another wave drenched him. He gasped for breath as the water gushed up into his mouth. The last thing he saw before he blacked out was Poseidon standing over him, looking thunderous, and water swirling out from the palm of his hand.

Zara held the Helm of Shadows under her arm, and fingered the Crystal Trident, leaning back against a tree trunk, with Astra resting his head beside her. She had made her way back to Artemis' forest, and had found Astra waiting for her at the tree hut. She had felt slightly guilty over stealing Hades' helmet, but it now cooled under her fingers, like it was meant to be with her. The Trident was sharp and edgy, though, and had already grazed her fingers numerous times.

She glanced at the pocket of her cloak, and decided to try an experiment. She quietly slipped the end of the Trident into the pocket. It fit, so she pushed it down further. To her amazement and pleasure, it didn't poke out the other end of the pocket, but continued to delve deeper into the folds. The top of the Trident disappeared entirely, and the pocket was still the same size as before. Zara paused for a second in wonder before sliding the Helm in as well.

Now, she had four different weapons of the gods. She had the Helm, the Trident, the Master Bolt in pieces, and the point of Athena's spear. But she knew that wasn't enough for what she was planning. She was going to have to visit some more Gods and Goddesses.

Standing up, Zara clutched at the hood of the cloak, which shimmered into view at her touch. She pulled the hood back and walked out of the forest, Astra trotting along behind her. The dagger at her belt felt light compared to the other heavy weapons she now possessed.

The sand and liquid paths lay before her. Zara wondered which direction to go: to Ares' warplane, or Apollo's chariot? To Aphrodite's palace, or back to Hephaestus' forge?

Zara shook her head. She wasn't going to choose those people yet. They came last, for they were the most dangerous. She looked down at Astra, who was wagging his tail eagerly, a knowing look in his eyes.

"Come on, Astra. Take me somewhere new," Zara smiled at the keen wolf.

Astra raced off, turning here, stopping there. Zara wound around behind him, her curly hair trailing. Astra finally stopped before a single cloud of the purest white. He nodded towards it, and then jumped on it.

Zara expected him to fall through it, but he disappeared as his paw touched the fluffy, clear surface. Zara rolled her eyes, exasperated. How many different magic ways did the Gods and Goddesses use just to move from place to place? Calmly, she stepped onto the cloud, and was transported someplace else.

CHAPTER EIGHT

Kind or Condescending?

Zara opened her eyes to the purest of whites, and bright, blinding light. After blinking a couple of times, her eyes adjusted. She was sitting on a floating cloud. Astra was lying down beside her, looking up at her lazily.

"Well, I took you somewhere new. What are you going to do?" his eyes asked.

Zara stood up, and found herself looking out at a sea of white clouds, each one floating, bobbing up and down slightly in an imaginary breeze. Right in front there was a vast, palace rising before her, carved from the clearest, smoothest marble, with swirls of purples and blues.

There weren't any doors or windows. None that were visible, at least. There was a little recorder and speaker in the marble, though, with a green, bejewelled button. Zara pressed it nervously.

Nothing happened.

Suddenly, the speaker crackled to life. "Haven of Hera. How may Her Majesty serve you?"

Zara rolled her eyes. The voice was placid and boring. A guard, no doubt, was waiting on the other side of the marble slab for an answer.

"I am Zara, Goddess of... something, I don't know what yet. I wish to speak with Her Majesty," Zara answered, pressing down the green button to transmit her voice.

There was a pause. "You do not know your title?"

"Is that not what I said? Open up! I must speak with Her Majesty!" Zara snapped impatiently.

The speaker died into silence. Then the marble slid away smoothly, and a man dressed in purple, blue and white greeted her solemnly.

"If you speak to Her Majesty like that, she will not be impressed. Please remove your shoes before entering," the guard said coldly. He looked stiff and insulted.

Zara slid off her boots and stepped inside. The interior of the palace was grand. It was lined with silver and white gold, with blooming lilies of different shades of blues and purples. There were vases studded with amethysts and sapphires, and the odd gleaming diamond.

Astra padded in after Zara, looking from side to side. The guard sniffed in disapproval and scrunched up his face, watching Astra leave smudged black paw prints on the fine floor. "Please make sure your dog does not destroy anything. Everything inside here is priceless. Take care," he sniffed.

Zara frowned at him. "Astra is a wolf, not a dog! Be respectful. You needn't look down on everything."

The guard's lips stretched into a grudging smile. "I must be pleasant. I must be inviting," he muttered under his breath, still holding the grimace.

Zara scowled further at hearing this. "Which way to Her Majesty?"

The guard pointed ahead in the direction Zara was facing. "Go through the marble doors and to your left. She is in her throne room."

Zara stalked off without a word of thanks. The guard glared after her, then abruptly turned away.

"Up to no good," he murmured. "That girl is up to no good."

Zara pushed open the doors of marble swirls and turned to face her left. There was a clear archway leading to a round room with millions of different purple and blue flowers, all studded with gems and painted with silver on the outlines. Zara ran over and stopped just after passing under the arch.

An immense cloud of peace stole over Zara's mind. She tried to resist the dreamy spell, but realised, too late, that if she was going to get a representative sample of Hera's power, she'd have to divert her into walking someplace else, or give it willingly. She wasn't about to break the peace now that a spell had taken hold of her.

A lady sitting on a throne of white marble, carved into the floor, was directly in front of Zara. She wore a purple headdress with amethysts and blue sequins studded into the embroidery. A dress of silvery satin was flowing down over her shoes, and a necklace of lapis lazuli and sapphire hung around her neck. Many silver bracelets were clamped onto her wrists, and her face was painted with swirls of purple, blue and white, on her cheeks and over her eyes.

This woman was obviously Hera. Her beautiful face stretched into a sad smile. "Come forth, One of Peace. No harm comes in the throne room of Hera."

Zara immediately broke the spell within her mind, rebelling against it. What she had come to do mattered more than admiring the beauty of Hera and her many flowers.

"Your Majesty." Zara politely bowed.

Hera seemed confused by this. "Men bow, young girl, not women! Curtsy with what skirts you have!"

Zara dropped down in a curtsy, but she looked up from beneath her lashes as she did. Hera was watching her intensely, with a curious expression on her face.

"What do you seek, young Goddess? My blessing? Protection? An answer?" Hera asked, once Zara had straightened.

Zara thought about it. Neither of the first two suggestions concerned her goal. But answers... that sounded tempting. She hadn't got to know much about herself. Perhaps Hera knew the answer?

"O Hera, I seek answers, for I have many questions," Zara said carefully.

"Ask away," was the reply from Hera.

"I do not truly know who I am. Your late husband, Zeus, did not supply me with much information." Zara kept her voice level.

Hera smiled slightly. "I'm afraid I do not know much about you either, my dear, only that you were found by Aphrodite. She says she found you in a bird's nest in her garden, but I think this is just another one of her typical lies. But tell me, what have you have found out about yourself?"

Zara opened her palm, revealing the fragments of Zeus's electric spear that she had retrieved from the cloak pocket. "That does not matter. I have made a plan to bring back your husband. It involves theft from the other Gods and Goddesses. I can only take something from you if you give it to me willingly, for otherwise this plan will not work."

Hera's eyes widened at seeing the fragments. "You... you have the Master Bolt! But how?"

By the glint in Zara's eye, Hera's question was answered. "Will you give me a gift, Lady Hera, so your husband may rise again? Or are you another of the people set out against him?"

Hera gulped and reached into a pocket. Bringing out her hand, there was a deep purple gem, smooth as the marble of the palace and shiny as glass. "It was mined out of one of the Greek mines. After finding it, one of my apprentices brought it back to me as a gift. Now I give it to you."

Zara took the gem and put it in her cloak's pocket. "Thank you, Lady Hera."

Suddenly, all the flowers in the room rippled. They seemed to grow tiny faces within their petals. Hera smiled and hushed them by touching the necklace at her throat.

"I apologise. Usually, the flowers will sound the alarm over theft. If you take a gem from any of the rooms, the flowers will know. But do not worry, they will not harm you. You leave now with my blessing, Untitled One," Hera explained, her eyes shining.

Zara nodded and left the room, turning back into the entrance hall. The guard was eyeing her suspiciously.

"You have a gem from Lady Hera. You have not been attacked by the flowers. Why?" he asked.

Zara smiled and didn't reply. Opening the marble slab again, she disappeared out onto the clouds.

CHAPTER NINE

Allies and Enemies

Back on the sand and shell paths, Zara clutched the gem in her hand worriedly. The place had changed. And not for the good of her cause.

There were guards everywhere, wearing scaly chain mail, holding spears made of sharp shells and grains of the whitest sand. Their faces looked as if they were carved from dry, hard coral of different colours, and their helmets had different animal carvings on them. It didn't look like anyone would get past them without inspection.

Zara looked down at Astra. "Distract them. I need to get to Aphrodite. Hurry."

Zara curled the cloak over her head and tied it up tightly. She put the gem away into the cloak pocket and watched Astra trot over to the closest guard. He barked loudly and threateningly, and the guard spun around in surprise.

"Hey, Starfish. One of Artemis' dear wolves. They don't usually leave the forest," the guard called to his neighbour.

The guard called Starfish frowned. "Strange... Perhaps it's telling you something, Turtle. Do we need Shark to translate?"

Turtle nodded in agreement. "He does seem distressed. You call for Shark whilst I calm him down. Shark only translates if the animal is negotiable."

As this conversation continued, Zara took the path past Starfish and started to run on the tips of her toes, so as to make no noise. Astra, hearing her pass, suddenly bolted and followed. The guards shouted for him to return, but by then he and Zara were long gone around a corner.

Zara looked up at the tall palace in front of her. It was carved of the purest crystal and diamond, with jagged edges and no ledges. There were many windows and open doors, without any guards.

"Aphrodite must be a real blonde to be this trusting," Zara observed sourly. Nothing seemed to have any sense of security.

Astra looked off to the side, away from Zara. Zara followed his eyes and saw a tall fountain with gardens surrounding it. Aphrodite was sitting amongst some lilies with a watering can and wearing magenta gardening gloves.

"There she is! But what of hers represents her power? I mean, love and beauty aren't a thing you can take from someone. Any suggestions, Astra?" Zara asked, clutching the Trident hard.

Astra shook his head. Zara sighed and started over to Aphrodite. As she approached, Aphrodite stiffened and turned around. Seeing Zara, she smiled and relaxed her tense shoulders.

"Welcome to my garden, Zara. Beautiful, is it not?" Aphrodite's eyes shone with fondness.

Zara nodded and knelt down beside her. "Aphrodite, I have something important to speak with you about."

"I know about how you stole Poseidon's Trident. But don't worry, I'm on your side. You needn't be anxious, as I will defend you if he comes this way," Aphrodite cut in.

"That isn't it, though I'm glad to hear you've sided with me," Zara said, waves of gratitude washing over her tense, alert mind.

"Then what is it?" Aphrodite enquired.

"Do you have anything that you can give to me that represents true love, or natural beauty?" Zara asked. "I need it to bring back Zeus."

Aphrodite sucked in a hissing breath. "To bring back Zeus? Doing deals with the residents of Hades?"

"Mmmm, that's not exactly it. I am finding Poseidon not fit to rule, and nor is Hades, for they are both weak in the role of leadership and do not have a firm grip on making the right decisions. Poseidon may be trying to be just, but he has already lost Artemis and Apollo from his side. Hades would be harsh with his punishments and not care for the small complaints and issues of others. Poseidon is too stubborn, and Hades is too rash."

At this, Aphrodite raised her eyebrows. Zara suddenly realised what she had said and blushed for her stupidity. Why had she spoken so freely? What was it about Aphrodite that made her trust her so completely?

"You... Why do you say this? You seem to understand others' qualities, bad and good, very well. Why?" Aphrodite questioned.

Zara reddened further. "I just... see people's weak points and strong points, and what people should improve on. I am too blunt, though, and sometimes say things too cruelly."

Aphrodite smiled knowingly. "You are wise, for your age. Kind and compassionate, too, but you hide that with your sharp tongue and metal mind. That is why I apologise."

Zara blinked and looked at Aphrodite. "What for?"

"Poseidon has been listening to every word you have been saying." Aphrodite tapped her ear and Zara saw a little starfish squirm under the touch of her finger. Zara hadn't noticed the tiny accessory. "Guards are on the way now."

Zara stood to run, but Aphrodite grabbed her ankle and held her fast. "I am sorry, dear. But Zeus has never given me enough attention."

Zara gritted her teeth. "Why betray him? Why?"

Aphrodite shrugged. "Poseidon offered me a giant bath and facial kit if I were to succeed in capturing you. I need those supplies, dear. I've been running out and my apprentices have been a little slack on doing my shopping for me."

Zara reached down and yanked at a long lock of Aphrodite's blonde hair. Aphrodite hissed in pain. "If that is all you wanted, you really are a blonde." Zara pulled harder and the Goddess shrieked in pain, scratching at her tormentor's hands.

Zara snatched away her hand and stomped on Aphrodite's fingers, making her let go. Dashing back towards Astra, Zara tightly clutched the small, heart-shaped clip she had tugged from Aphrodite's hair. She could hear the loud footsteps of guards approaching.

Astra snarled as the guards rounded the corner. The first guard stopped, and waved out his hands.

"Starfish, Turtle, is this the dog you saw before?" he asked.

Starfish nodded. "Yeah, Shark. This is the one."

"It seems to be with Aphrodite. It is telling us the Godling has gone round the other side," Shark explained.

Turtle smiled, his jagged teeth scraping his dry, patchy, coral skin. "Parrotfish and Eel will catch her. We may as well go back to our posts."

Shark grumbled. "I wish I was one of the Eel squads."

"But you're lucky, Shark! All sharks can translate. Starfish can only poison people, and turtles are so common. You got a lucky break. You should be proud of your squadron," Turtle exclaimed.

Shark sighed. "But Eels can use the electric shock shells and concussion bombs. Those are so cool!"

As the pointless conversation went on, Zara snuck past and Astra trotted past the guards, and they did not even notice either of them passing.

Zara, relieved for her safety, put the hairpin away in the magical pocket. "Two more Gods to go, Astra, and I fear they will be the hardest. Ares, and Apollo."

Astra grinned wolfishly. He barked loudly and cocked his head towards Ares' warplane.

Zara bit her lip. She had hoped to approach Ares last, as she had a few bones to pick with him. But then again, Apollo still seemed to think he had a fight to finish with her, so in some ways, he was far more dangerous than Ares.

Zara began to approach the warplane, but a voice behind her stopped her in her tracks. She couldn't recognise it, but it sounded somewhat familiar.

"We have advice for you, dear Goddess of Justice. Please stop and hear us out."

Zara turned and saw two beautiful women, one much younger than the other. It was the younger one who had spoken, because she was smiling kindly and had spread her arms wide. She was dressed in a long, green silk dress with flowers all over her fingers and entangled in her bouncy, voluminous hair. Her eyes were like bright daisies and her skin was golden, with freckles across her nose. She seemed to be in her late twenties.

The elder of the two was wearing a short, yellow dress with golden leaves and a crown of thorns, wheat and corn upon her head. She was dark skinned and had glassy green eyes that clashed with her white-blonde frizzy hair, highlighted under the sun. She looked as if she was in her fifties, and still beautiful.

The older woman looked blank and confused, staring at Zara inquiringly. "Is this truly your child? She looks nothing like you! Her powers may be related, but she looks more like Aphrodite than anyone else."

The younger frowned at her companion, who was seemingly her mother. "She is my child! I can tell by the strong bond between us."

"Excuse me?" Zara asked, stepping towards the women, "Who are you? What do you want?"

The woman in yellow looked back at Zara. "We seek nothing from you. I am Demeter, Goddess of Corn and the Harvest. This is my daughter, Persephone, who is the Queen of the Underworld, and a Goddess. She believes she has finally found her daughter. That is, you."

Persephone looked delighted. "It is really you, Zaralapizina? It is, isn't it? You were born just as beautiful as you are now..." She reached out and stroked Zara's face.

Zara flinched away, and stepped back. "If you are my mother, then what is my title?"

Persephone's face lit up further, and she seemed to glow with pride. "You are the Goddess of Justice, Absorption and Understanding. Is that what you wanted to know?"

Zara felt immobile, and shocked. "How do you know?" Zara herself was not sure whether this was the truth, but it did match the conclusion she had been coming to herself.

Demeter cut in. "We Goddesses have our ways of knowing things. Now that this little family reunion is over, I have something to say to you."

Zara suddenly felt a pang of panic. "What? Are you with Poseidon? Are you going to take me to him?"

Demeter snorted. "That cuttlefish should never have laid a finger on that throne. Zeus may not have been very good at justice, but since you'd come, I thought perhaps you could change him. Unfortunately, you were put under the biased influence of Artemis and now Poseidon rules. We are on your side. We wish for your rule to go ahead."

Persephone's eyes sparkled. "And then I am free to wander here without anyone preaching over me! Hades will be so pleased that we can finally always be together, all year round!"

"Hades? What of him? He is my master, yes, but what does he have to do with you?" Zara asked, mystified.

"Hades is my husband," Persephone explained, "For a long time I have been stuck in the Underworld with him, only let out for six months of the year. Now I am allowed to walk the surface of earth whenever I please! All thanks to you freeing Hades. I am ever grateful to you, my daughter."

Demeter rolled her eyes. "I really don't see what you find in that man. He is so feisty and quick to anger. How can you stand him?"

Persephone glared up at her mother. "Because he is easy to talk to, and understands me! He is always calm when I am around, unless something really displeases him."

Zara felt like her brain was starting to freeze up. She had been dumped with so much information and no explanations! Did she really have to ask all the questions?

Demeter, seeing her annoyed expression, smiled knowingly. "You are the child of Hades and Persephone. She calls herself Goddess of Flowers and such, but she really has nothing to do with it. Now, what else do you need to know?"

Zara's eyes bulged. "What do you mean, what else do I need to know? An explanation! Why? Why?"

Demeter frowned. "I don't know what you mean by 'Why' but anyway–"

Persephone cut her mother off. "You see, Hades did not tell you this because he did not know! I gave birth to you in secret and left you on a lily pad in the garden of Aphrodite for her to find you and assume you had been born from one of her magnificent flowers. Hades would not have been able to tolerate you as a child. He would have taught you to hate the Gods and would have twisted your view of justice, which is one of your primary powers. I could not allow that. You are too important to the future of the Gods. You will teach us how to be civil and empathetic. You are a Goddess of the new age."

Zara put her head in her hands, massaging her temples, trying to take this information in. It was believable and there was evidence and information to back up the case. It was hard to believe, though, suddenly being filled with knowledge like this.

Zara lifted her head suddenly. "So you are saying I am your daughter, an immortal Goddess, with powers of Justice, Absorption and Understanding, the child of the God of Hell and with a special part to play for the future of the Gods."

Persephone nodded, looking enchanted with joy. Demeter looked tired but relieved, and turned and began to walk away.

"Come, Persephone. We must tend to the crops of the people. They await our good fortune," Demeter called over her shoulder. Persephone sighed and hurried away after her.

Zara glared after them. "And I didn't even get something to add to my collection."

Looking around, Zara realised that Astra had disappeared. She spun around wildly and spotted the wolf chewing on a strand of wheat, with a flower lying close beside him. Zara smiled thankfully. She tugged the wheat from Astra's mouth, placing it in the cloak pocket along with everything else and twined the flower behind her ear.

Now, that our little delay is over, off to Ares with a little less spite packed up my sleeve. I realise that he probably thought he was doing the right thing, Zara thought.

She was still confused with her new name. It sounded as if someone had tried to add a 'lapis lazuli' to her name randomly. Strange and weird as it was, it suited the fact that she was a Goddess, and all the Gods and Goddesses seemed to have peculiar, tangled names.

Astra barked impatiently and trotted over to the warplane. Zara darted behind him, opened the door of the plane and let herself inside. The moment she had passed the doorframe she found herself on the ground with a hand holding her head down with heavy breathing just beside her ear.

CHAPTER TEN

Aided or Alone?

"What is your business here, deceiver and thief? Not to steal any of my ornaments, I hope!" Ares hissed, pushing her head harder against the cold metal of the floor.

"Ow! Stop it! Is that any way to treat your better? Unhand me at once!" Zara exclaimed.

As Zara had suspected, this made Ares push harder. The angrier she made him, the easier it would be to deceive him and take an object.

"Guard your sharp tongue and keep your trap shut! 'Your better', my Aunt Petunia! Don't be such an arrogant witch," Ares mimicked, his face going red.

Zara grinned up at him. "You are so easy to reel in, Ares. You rise for every piece of bait you are offered, even if the fish is small."

Ares was confused, due to his thick head. He didn't really understand metaphorical comments very well. "Whaddaya mean by that? I ain't no fish rising to bait! See? No fins, no gills!"

Taking advantage of Ares' confusion, Zara kicked with all her might and left Ares sprawled on the floor, panting heavily. She jumped up and sped over to a rack of weapons, which held spears, axes, darts, arrows, daggers and swords. She plucked a stiletto and matching scabbard from the throng of sharp objects and stowed it in the cloak pocket. Quickly, Zara dashed out the door and slammed it behind her. She heard Ares throw it open with a slam.

"Come back here right now, you ignorant little girl! Return to me what is mine!" Ares roared after her, but didn't follow her. He didn't really care, anyhow, but wanted to make a scene. After all, he was the God of War.

Zara barely listened. She was too intent on getting away and finding Apollo. He was the last one she needed to visit. And time was of the essence.

Then Zara stopped. She just sat down, and thought. Astra whined in surprise and sat down beside her, staring at her inquisitively.

Zara stared back. "I don't know what I'm going to do when I see Apollo, Astra. I don't know what thing of his that represents his power to take without burning myself. He is the God of the Sun, after all."

Astra tossed his head in frustration. "You actually believe that is his only power?" he seemed to say.

Zara nodded, understanding. "Well, he did say he's God of the Prophecy too. But prophecies come from the other world, the future. It's no use trying to find something that represents the future."

Zara suddenly became aware of footsteps coming from before her. A pair of winged sandals appeared before her, and she looked up. A man wearing a traditional Greek robe, a winged helmet and winged sandals stood before her. He was pale, with smoky grey eyes; salt-and-pepper hair and he had a lyre stuck under one arm.

"I am Hermes, messenger of the Gods. I'm also the God of Theft. I have a message for you from the God of the Wild, Pan, noting your bravery and so on," Hermes said impatiently, waving a letter out to Zara.

Zara snatched the letter. "Thank you for your service."

Zara went to open the letter, and then realised Hermes was still watching, waiting. Zara looked up at him again and raised an eyebrow. "Ah, yes?"

Hermes held out his hand. "Tip."

Zara nodded with sudden knowledge. "Ah... right, you want some money. Sorry, don't have any on me."

Hermes now looked furious. "No money? Do you take me for Iris? I don't do free fares!"

Zara shrugged. "Sorry, nothing I can do about it, Wingman. I do have a valuable gem, but I need that for more important matters. And who is Iris?"

Ignoring the last question, Hermes seemed to understand. He nodded and looked slightly disappointed. When Zara saw the spark in his eye, she rolled back, just in time as Hermes lunged to grab her collar.

"Deceiver!" Zara spat, "You ought to be ashamed. Trying to harm one as innocent and harmless as me!"

Hermes burst out laughing. "You, innocent and harmless! You are a common liar, like me. You've been convicted of stealing. You ought to be my apprentice, but Hades has already plucked the only sweet grape of the bunch."

Zara stood up and brushed herself off. "It's not likely you're going to be much more help, but I do ask a favour of you."

Hermes' eyes glinted with suspicion. "And what will you give me in return?"

"Double the tips I owe you, plus some wings." Zara didn't know how she'd be able to pull this off, but she figured there would be some way or other.

Hermes looked tempted, despite desperately trying to hide it. "And if you fail to supply me with these objects?"

"I don't know. I'll be your slave for a day, send messages, whatever! You haven't even heard how simple my favour is!" Zara snapped, now extremely agitated. "All I want is a souvenir that represents your powers."

"Here," Hermes pulled a letter opener from his pocket, "Take this. I'm a messenger, and I stole this from Pan last time I saw him while he was sealing the letter he sent you. All the more fitting; I earnt it through theft."

Zara took the letter opener and put it in the cloak pocket. "Thank you. I will repay the debt as soon as possible."

Hermes smiled. "You'd better, or I'll start charging interest!"

He disappeared in a shower of letters, leaving Zara to wonder at the crumpled missive in her hands. She sliced open the envelope with her dagger and pulled out the contents. She began to read.

> *Dear Zaralapizina,*
>
> *I congratulate you on your bravery for facing off the new King of Gods, putting others before yourself and being ever so cautious.*
>
> *I knew you from when you were a child because, during the six months of her leave, Persephone told me about you and that if I were to find you, I would give you to her right away. Unfortunately, plans went wrong and Aphrodite depended on Ares for help.*

> *Here is a token of my gratitude to know you are following what you believe to be right.*
>
> *Thanks,*
>
> *Pan, God of the Wild*
>
> *PS Those panpipes work only for a worthy owner.*

Zara shook the envelope and a set of reed panpipes fell out, clattering onto the dry sand. Zara picked the instrument up, inspecting it to see whether it was trapped or tricked with magic, but found no evident clue that anything untoward was contained inside.

Zara lifted the pipes to her lips and tried to blow, but only a short whistle came out. It was a start, but she figured she'd have to be more worthy to play an actual note.

Suddenly the hairs on the back of Zara's neck prickled. She heard the clattering of footsteps and voices. Astra growled in warning as the coral guards came round a corner, spotted her and quickened their pace.

"It's her! The thief, the traitor! Get the girl! Get her!" one guard shouted. The others stormed behind him. Zara felt a surge of panic and turned to run, then thought the better of it.

She turned back to face the guards. When they were in earshot, she called out to them. "Yes, this way! She went this way! Follow me!"

The guards halted, confused. "Aren't you the witch?!" one yelled.

Zara shook her head and gave a short laugh. "No, I'm one of Artemis' apprentices. She gave me this cloak for my handy archery. No wonder, it's supposed to make me blend in! Sorry for the mistake."

The guards scratched their heads. "How'd you get here? What business do you have with the Gods?"

Zara winked. "I've got a message to give to Apollo from Artemis. Don't worry, I was just on my way now. I have to say, I'm a bit lost. Could you direct me to him?"

One guard nodded. "Third to your right, straight forward, then your third right again. I'd bring sun block, if I were you."

The guards roared with laughter. Then one stopped and stepped forward. "We'd best be on our way now. Still got to find that brat of a Godling that needs imprisonment. Which way did you say she went?"

"Straight ahead, toward the palace. She laughed and told me she was going to dethrone Poseidon. She's probably already there by now, and sitting upon the throne. She is very powerful, after all..."

Zara smiled as the guards sped past her in pursuit of the lie she had laid out. She giggled and started off towards her new destination. Astra padded along beside her, looking alert.

"Go track the guards, put them off the scent. That translator should be with them, so tell him that I'm somewhere random and far away," Zara ordered.

Astra turned and bolted after the guards. When he was out of sight, Zara ran in her own direction.

CHAPTER ELEVEN

Safety and Danger

Third right, straight, third right again. Zara frowned when she found an empty piece of land covered in dry, crisp brown grass. It crunched under her feet as she walked around, searching for Apollo.

"Nothing," Zara muttered. "I've been led on a wild goose chase. Most likely a trap. I guess they weren't fooled by me."

No guards came thundering down the paths. It was only a matter of time, though.

But somehow Zara didn't really feel this way; it was just an excuse for her puzzled mind. She didn't have an answer to her own question, and this was making her jump to conclusions.

A faint whirring above her head made Zara look up, then suddenly shade her eyes as a blinding, searing light hit them. Even when her eyes were closed, the light still filtered through, filling her sight with a blood red haze.

"Turn around, you fool! If you don't, you'll never see again!" a voice roared. Zara recognised it as Apollo's, now rough and commanding.

Zara turned and buried her face in her hands, feeling some of the hairs on her neck start burning and scorching off her skin. The smell of smoke wafted around the ring of brown grass, which was probably burning, too.

Suddenly, the heat switched off, and Zara felt the pouring, ceaseless light stop burdening her back. She lifted her head and opened her eyes, letting some dim sunlight flow through. She could see nothing but black ashes wherever there had been grass.

"So, you've finally come to apologise for your arrogant behaviour before? Or is that just wishful thinking?" Apollo said behind her, seemingly tired.

Zara spun around and shot Apollo the dirtiest look she could, mustering up all the loathing, disgust, revulsion and repulsion she felt towards him into one facial expression.

"You are such a superior, authoritative, imbecilic jerk. Never expect an apology from me."

"And yet you come here asking me for a token to represent my powers?" Apollo smirked sarcastically. He was standing next to his chariot, which was emitting low levels of heat. He was rubbing it with his bare hands, sneering at Zara. Zara wondered how his hands weren't dropping off from the heat.

"How did you know my purpose for being here?" Zara asked warily.

"First of all, news spreads between us Gods. Well, except for the Gods who are more distant, like Hephaestus or Hecate. Second of all, it's written all over your face. You want something and you're impatient to get it. So then, I'll hurry up for you. Here." Apollo tossed a tiny glass orb at Zara, which she fumbled to catch.

Zara inspected the glass orb. "What is it?"

Apollo smiled teasingly. "A crystal orb, you ninny. It can predict snippets of the future. This one is so small, it'll probably work about three times."

Zara now looked at the transparent ball with disinterest. "So that's all. You give me something that only weakly represents your powers. You know, you're so cold. You can hold a grudge for a long time."

"It's been about the time span of a day in human hours. That's not very long," Apollo protested.

"But you're holding it over something stupid. I beat you, and gave you advice. I considered you as an equal, for I, too, am not perfect. No one is. Not even a God as powerful as you."

Apollo stared at her for a moment, then turned abruptly and went back to rubbing his chariot. Zara's eyes widened as she realised a vital fact.

"Ah, I see now!" Zara cried, bursting into laughter.

Apollo looked over his shoulder in surprise, and a little bit of interest.

"You are the most timid, shy and insecure person I have ever met, Apollo! You hide your shyness with jokes and puns at others to stop them from viewing you as broken and closed. You want people to think of you as perfect, a role model, a superior! But really, you just want to hide your cowardly, insecure self from others." Zara laughed again.

Apollo looked irritated. "How dare you accuse me of such–"

"There really is no use hiding it now, Apollo. Once people find out, there'll be no convincing them otherwise," Zara said, suddenly serious. "Now you're just covering your anxiousness with anger."

Apollo opened his mouth to retort, then gave a little sigh and sat down, fiddling with his golden sword. "You're right. If the other Gods do find out about this, though, I'll never hear the end of their jokes and teasing. I thought that if I hid my fears, everyone would look up to me, not look down. No wonder Artemis is so highly favoured over me on Earth. I don't go on important quests. I sit around and clean my chariot all day. You've been the first piece of action I've had in years. I enjoyed sparring with you, but I didn't want you to know. That is why I fought so ferociously for you to stay, so I could continue to fight with you. I didn't want to have to be stuck on my own again."

Zara frowned. "Then speak up! Talk with the Gods, organise meetings, be social! Don't be a spud and sit around all day. You know that if you want attention you have to earn it! Be proud of yourself and find your good qualities and shine them on others so they are drawn to you."

Apollo looked up at her blankly. "I suppose I could try that..."

"*Do*, not try! You must, and you will achieve your goals, or you will never get me off your back about it!" Zara snapped. "Now, I'm sure my little lecture here is at least worth one of your tokens. Other than this glass orb." She threw the orb at his feet.

Apollo fiddled around in his pocket and brought out a bottle of thick liquid gold with chunks of what looked like glass. "Here. Don't drink the gold stuff, but clean off the chunks of crystal and eat them and you can grant a wish. The gold stuff is a preservative, tastes gross and is like acid on the tongue. But the crystals are great medicine, and I only give it to worthy people. Be sure there's no gold on the crystal."

Zara took the bottle from his hands. "Thank you. But how does this represent your powers?"

Apollo laughed. "Not many people know this, but I am a skilled medicine maker. I experiment all the time when no one is around. This is merely one of my many creations."

Zara waved goodbye as she started back onto the sandy dunes. There seemed to be no guards about, and she had everything she needed. Now all she had to do was travel to Hephaestus' forge.

As she stepped out into the open, feeling good, shouts of "Grab her!" and "Get the little rat!" rang out. Before she could even begin to run, guards pounced upon her from all sides, seemingly melting out of the air. Zara shrieked and kicked and bit her attackers, but to no avail. One twisted her arms back and lifted her off the ground, and another grabbed her feet. Then they moved off, carrying her along between them.

What a fix! Zara thought, panicking. How on earth am I going to squirm out of this?

CHAPTER TWELVE

Lost or Found?

The guards had been carrying Zara for over thirty minutes when one groaned and dropped her on the ground, making her jolt awake from her sleepy trance and desperately try to scramble away, only to be grabbed by the ankles and hauled up again.

"No use trying to get away. We got you in a firm grasp," her captor snickered.

Another guard sounded aggravated. "Octopus, toughen up! You almost let the witch escape, you ninny! You would have brought shame on our squad!"

"I know, I apologize. I didn't mean to drop her, but I've been carrying her all this way and she got heavy. My back gave way, that's all," Octopus whined.

"Well, here's a trick. Shift the weight to the other hand every now and then! It helps," another guard barked.

"Talking about tricks, we caught this little blighter quite niftily, no?" another sniggered.

"No you did not!" Zara spat. "You attacked me from behind, which is a sign of cowardice and unfair play. You were invisible. Another move that's not in the rule book. You did not catch me niftily, you caught me using unfair play and superpowers. I didn't even have a chance to put up a fight, you stupid oafs!"

The guards all turned to look at her. "Shut up, girl. The point that matters is that we caught you, and you will now be sent to Tartarus at Lord Poseidon's wish. That is what we were sent to do. And we have accomplished our goal. We will be rewarded."

Zara snorted. "I doubt it. Poseidon will merely praise you in a cold tone and dismiss you, not letting you touch any of the treasures he hides away in his rooms. You will be sent away, miserable and empty-handed, with nothing to do but mock passers-by and run amok."

The guards went quiet. One kicked a shell by his foot despairingly.

Zara frowned. "Oh please. So you knew all along? What's the benefit for you?"

One guard burst. "He's pulled that exact same manoeuvre every time we achieve or triumph in something! He never ever paid us any attention, and he owes me seven weeks' wages!"

"Exactly. So what is the point of bringing me to him?" Zara said craftily.

A guard looked sullen. "Well, he did say you were causing trouble..."

Zara sniffed. "I am simply trying to bring back Zeus so he can claim his throne again. I know Poseidon is your master and all, but he sucks at ruling the place. If Zeus comes back, I can knock some sense into him and help him restore his place on the throne under certain conditions."

The guard called Octopus who had been carrying her spoke up. "But he'll punish us if we let you go!"

Zara nodded thoughtfully. "If you let me go, I'll try my best to get you a new job after Zeus rules again."

"But how do we know you'll keep your word?" Octopus asked doubtfully.

Zara went quiet. She didn't have any proof to show she would keep her promise. There was no way.

"Perhaps if she signs an oath? That way, she can't break it, unless she's got a death wish," one of the guards suggested. Harsh laughter broke out from the group.

"Would you mind informing me what an oath is?" Zara asked, perplexed to what the new word meant.

"But you are a Goddess! Surely you should know how to do simple magic tricks like an oath. You have to promise on something that is important to you. Then, if you do not fulfil the promise within the time limit given, we have the right to take that important thing from you. Whatever it is, the magic in the oath will give it to us," one of the guards explained.

Zara understood completely now, and the conditions sounded fair. "Then I swear on my powers that I will get you all new jobs as soon as Zeus is able to grant my wishes."

The guard dropped her feet, and they all walked off. Zara was left nursing her legs from being dropped on the hard, gravelly sand and glaring furiously after the guards.

Octopus turned and called back to her. "Don't forget, or you'll lose your powers!"

Zara didn't need reminding. She stood up and looked around, lost. She would need Astra's help to find her way back around. But Astra was off spying on guards and giving them false information. How would she get him to come?

Zara remembered in the forest how when Astra had wandered off, Artemis would blow hard on a tiny silver whistle to call him back. She didn't have the whistle now, but perhaps the pipes from Pan would do the trick. That was if she was worthy enough, though.

She pulled out the pipes and put them to her lips, then blew hard and loudly. A piercingly high note shrieked from the holes on the end. It wasn't a pleasant noise, so she guessed she still had some work to do.

Astra did not appear. No one did. So with that, with no help at all, Zara wandered off, lost in a maze of paths, not knowing where to go.

CHAPTER THIRTEEN

Old and New

Zara stopped in front of a significant patch of weeds next to the sandy path. She had been past here before. She must be going in circles.

"This is not fun at all," Zara muttered, crossing her arms. "I wish I weren't so lost."

"Ha ha! You wish!" A woman's voice laughed from behind her. Zara turned, but no one was there.

"Behind you!" the voice called out again, this time even more teasing. Zara frowned and spun round, but still saw no one. The voice yelled out again and again, and Zara continued turning around on the spot until she was so frustrated she snapped.

"Make yourself visible, you annoying prat! If this is amusing to you, it is not for me! Never laugh at a person, but with them! This is a cruel and unfair joke," Zara yelled, turning a full circle.

"Find me if you can!" the voice jeered, and Zara sighed angrily.

She sat down, seemingly admitting defeat. Quietly, ever so quietly, she unscrewed the lid of Apollo's jar and picked out a crystal, wiping off the golden sludge with her fingers. Once she was sure it was clean, she slipped it into her mouth and swallowed.

Instantly, her mind cleared, and she could see the woman clearly. She was clad in black, wearing a thick black overcoat, large black boots and a tight-fitting black body suit. Her face was pale, and her lips were black, and she wore black eyeliner and black mascara. Her hair was long and flowing and, you guessed it, it was black as night.

The woman sneered. "So you now see me. Your eyes are not clouded to my magic."

Zara looked at the beautiful lady in annoyance. "You were irritating me, witch. Now, would you mind explaining yourself?"

The gothic woman was still sneering, and dropped into a mocking curtsey. "I am Hecate, Goddess of Black Magic. I love to play tricks on the blind."

Zara felt a flare of fire rise within her. "I am not blind, but I did not know! It was simply lack of knowledge that barred my way!"

Hecate laughed again, a screeching cackle like a crow makes in the morning. "Ha ha! Knowledge must be everything to you. Now you will be able to see me forever more. That is not fair. Oh well."

"Well then, what represents magic?" Zara asked impatiently.

Hecate paused. "I don't know. I guess existence is a kind of magic in itself. I mean, magic is simply an extraordinary way of using science."

"Thank you. Now, would you mind directing me to Hephaestus' forge? I'm afraid I'm quite lost," Zara asked, thinking about the information she'd just been given.

"Don't worry, I'll help you. Stand still. This may hurt a little, since you're being yanked through different dimensions to get to your destination," warned Hecate, then she curved her wrist and clicked her fingers.

Zara felt the blood rush to her head as she twisted through different places, worlds, and universes. It was uncomfortable, and there was a throbbing pain in her fingers. She closed her eyes, hopefully to block out the strange scenery, but she felt a singeing pain in her temples. She instantly stopped moving and waited for time to pass. One, two, three, four, five, six...

Zara fell forwards, suddenly released back into gravity. The suspension that been holding her up snapped, and she dropped to the floor, quickly putting her hands out to stop herself from taking a major spill.

"Hello again, Godling. What are you here for?" the gruff but friendly voice of Hephaestus asked from ahead of her.

Zara stood and brushed herself off, grinning at the mellow giant.

"It seems you have many more possessions since you left here, Godling. Show me the fine creations you have obtained," Hephaestus said knowingly.

Zara let the contents of the cloak pocket scatter onto the wooden floorboards. Hephaestus' eyes bulged as he looked at each object, admiring its uniqueness. He was even more surprised when Zara pulled out the Helm of Shadows and Crystal Trident from the folds of her cloak, and threw the pieces of the Master Bolt onto the ground with the other belongings. Finally, she untied the cloak and tossed it at Hephaestus' feet.

"You are a fine thief, Godling, but what do you expect me to do with all these?" Hephaestus quizzed.

Zara looked at him, then took a hammer from nearby and offered it to him. "You are the God of the Forge, Hephaestus. Will you make Zeus a new weapon, and help bring him back to life?"

Hephaestus worked for the rest of the day, melding the objects together. He had first shown Zara to a spare room with few luxuries. It had a wooden bed, a fire, a stool with a cushion and a chest to place her belongings in. Zara had taken a rug and sat down on it in front of the fire, dozing off from weakness and exhaustion.

When she awoke, she was no longer lying on the floor, but on the mattress of her wooden bed. Someone was sitting on the stool beside her, watching her wake up. That person had probably been watching her whilst she slept too... but just who was this person?

Zara rubbed her eyes and sat up, blinking sleep out of her eyes. Everything that had been blurry suddenly came into focus.

There was a man next to her on the stool with black curly hair, a goatee and sparkling lavender eyes. He wore a purple t-shirt and mauve jeans, with big black boots on his feet. He looked troublesome and audacious, and appeared to be in his mid-twenties.

"Finally awake. You must've been very tired to sleep for two whole days. Now, to introduce myself; I am Dionysus, God of Wine and Grapes and Alcohol, and all the rest that's related to that stuff," he explained.

Zara frowned. "It seems I forgot to ask you for something that represents your powers."

Dionysus laughed. "Oh well, you don't know much history. I've done you a couple of favours over the last day or so. One of them will probably overjoy you, the other is just news. I found your wolf sniffing around my vineyard, so I guessed I'd better return him."

Astra trotted into the room at his mention, looking around. When he saw Zara, he barked happily and leapt onto the bed, his tail wagging and his tongue lolling out of his mouth.

"Get off me, Astra! You're slobbering on me!" Zara protested. Astra ignored the request and curled up on her stomach and closed his eyes.

Dionysus smiled. "Second piece of news is that Hephaestus has finished creating the new 'weapon' you ordered him to make. It is quite splendid. Would you like to see it?"

Zara pushed Astra off, sat up and leaned forward eagerly. "Please, bring it in! I'm most keen to see the result."

Dionysus shouted something in Greek and Hephaestus marched in, an object smothered in a cloth lying in his brawny hands. "Here it is. It took me a long time to forge it, Godling, so I expect much thanks."

Hephaestus whipped off the cloth and Zara gasped.

A brilliant sceptre of pale metallic blue lay in his hands. A beautiful orb of glittering crystal was encrusted at the top, with sparkling amethysts and rose quartz. The staff itself was entwined with all sorts of different jewels and valuable substances. It was beyond stunning. It was truly exquisite.

Zara held her own hands out, then rethought and drew them back. "I cannot touch it. I will absorb it if I do so, and that would mean my mission was pointless. Do you still have any leftover objects?"

Hephaestus shook his head. "I used them all, as you asked. They've all been melted and moulded together to make the core of this sceptre. I guess its powers are beyond imagining now."

"Give me the staff with the cloth wrapped around it, please. That way, I can carry it around. And thank you, Hephaestus, for your hard work towards this," Zara acknowledged, getting up.

Hephaestus wrapped the cloth around the rod and handed it to Zara, who took it carefully, then walked out of the room, calling back her thanks once more.

CHAPTER FOURTEEN

Right or Wrong?

As soon as Zara was back in the fresh, salty air, a pang of worry stabbed at her mind. How would she get in contact with Zeus? How was she to bring him back to life? She no longer possessed the Helm of Shadows, for now it was a part of the sceptre.

A part of the sceptre...

Zara gasped and scolded herself for her foolishness. The object in her hands would bring back Zeus himself, for it had the powers of every God and Goddess she knew, apart from Dionysus, but she didn't need the power of alcohol in the rod.

She held the sceptre in front of herself, wondering how she would use it. She remembered Hecate's words. Magic is existence, a form of extraordinary science... And what was science but physics and chemistry? She had not studied science at all, but if science was just magic, then the rod should be used easily.

Zara focused on the staff, blocking out everything else. The staff seemed to sparkle, then the bright blue went a violent blood red and black, the colours of the Helm. Greek writing in golden ink appeared, and Zara read it slowly, not really understanding what she was reading but somehow knowing what it meant in her head all the same. Instantly, she was surrounded by the dimness, and everything was dark.

Zeus was there. He looked surprised to see her again, and with such an object.

"What do you hold, and why does it possess Hades' helmet's powers?" he asked.

"That story can wait. For now, I need you to co-operate. Hold the staff," Zara demanded.

Zeus looked confused, but he obeyed. He tried to get a proper grip, but his hand went through the object. He frowned. Zara rolled her eyes. "Put your hand around it. You don't have to actually touch it."

Zeus tried again, wrapping his fingers around the wand. Zara let go of the cloth, letting it drop, and placed her hand on the round orb on top. She uttered her wish under her breath and prayed to the Fates to let her plan work. She closed her eyes, hoping that when she opened them, she would be in the light again.

The orb grew warm, then searing hot. Zara pushed her hand down harder, gritting her teeth against the pain. *Please, oh please, let this work, she prayed, or everything I have done will have been for nothing. Please, take the ghost coin from me and use it to pay the debt I owe.*

Zara dared open one eye as the gem cooled down. As she had hoped, it was no longer dim and everything looked bright. The sceptre was blue-white again, and the golden writing was gone. And most of all, Zeus was standing before her, whole and alive.

Zeus looked bewildered. "How by the three Fates did you—"

Zara cut him off. "You owe me. A lot, in fact. Now, once you're back on the throne, I have a lot of favours to ask you of. I owe many other people things and you are my only hope to fulfil these promises. Now, come. We've got to go dethrone Poseidon."

"Why are you suddenly on my side?" Zeus asked cautiously.

"Because Poseidon sucks at ruling, and so will Hades if he earns the throne. I need you to be King of Gods again, but under certain conditions. I'll tell you those as soon as you're ruling," Zara answered, and walked off towards the palace.

There were no guards on the way, so Zara guessed Astra had distracted them well for the past two days.

When Zara got to the palace, she pushed open the double doors, marched in and over to the elevator. Zeus followed her in and she pressed the button. They sped upwards whilst the guards watching the doors simply stood and gaped like goldfish.

As they neared the top, Zara became impatient and forced open the doors, jumping and hauling herself up on the ledge. She waited until Zeus reached the top through the elevator and came out to follow her. He was holding the sceptre, as she had left it behind.

"We need Poseidon's Trident to get through into there," Zeus said bluntly, pointing at the locked door with the three holes.

Zara gripped the sceptre tightly through the cloth and knocked on the door three times, softly and slowly. Nothing happened for a moment, then, as she'd hoped, the door creaked open on its hinges.

Poseidon was snoring on his throne of water and bubbles, his eyes closed. He looked perfectly comfortable and content, not to mention, vulnerable. Zara knew better than to just waltz in, though, for he may be setting a trap.

Zeus, however, was not so smart. He was striding in, looking triumphant, when Hades leapt out from the shadows and fastened him in a grip of iron, a knife at his neck. Zeus choked and dropped the wand, letting it clatter to the floor. Zara stepped forwards to grab the sceptre but Hades spoke.

"Move another muscle and Zeus dies, girl," he snarled.

Zara watched him warily and froze. Hades wasn't himself. Poseidon had probably messed with his mind whilst she was away.

"Let him go, my lord. He's harmless without a weapon." Zara said quietly. Somehow, her smaller, quieter voice sounded more threatening and frightening than her angry hiss.

"As I have learnt, that is not true. Poseidon can create water from nothing. I'm sure that Zeus here can summon lightning at his own wish too. And if I'm right, you could use your powers if they were physical, not mental," Hades snapped.

Zara straightened her back. "Perhaps powers of wit are better than those of brawn. Perhaps powers of defence are better than those of offence."

With a quick darting movement, Zara grabbed Hades' dagger by the blade and yanked it out of his hand. Again, the metal blade melded into her palm and she was left uninjured. Zeus sprang forwards as soon as the knife was no longer threatening and grabbed the sceptre. He pointed it at Hades.

"Poseidon will have no chance to punish you if you let us return Zeus to the throne again. His powers will be restricted if you let us past to reach him," Zara reasoned. She lifted her chin proudly. "He will be no match for our weapon."

Hades eyed the rod with a new interest. "What does it do?"

"Everything," Zara shrugged, then pushed past Hades, Zeus at her side.

Zeus tapped Poseidon's head gently with the sceptre, and his snoring became louder. "There," he muttered, "Now he will not wake to disturb us."

With a team effort, they lifted Poseidon, who was still snoozing, from the throne.

Zeus settled down on the throne, and looked at Zara expectantly. "Well, say the words to enthrone me. We do not have all day."

Zara suddenly saw a hole in her plan. She did not know Ancient Greek. She did not know the words at all. What could she do in this situation when all she had worked for was only to be stopped at the last second?

She looked at Zeus desperately. "I don't know the words. Do you?"

Zeus rolled his eyes. "It's not as if I can enthrone myself, is it?"

Hades stepped forward and pushed Zara away. "I do. Let me do it, she still has much to learn."

Hades began to mutter in Ancient Greek. Zeus looked pleased as the statues returned to his form, and the throne went an electric blue. The walls solidified into gold again, and everything was back to how it had been before Poseidon took over.

Zeus sighed with joy. "Back to normal now. Thank you, brother. You two can both leave now."

Zara frowned. "I said I would have you enthroned under certain conditions, and if you granted me some wishes. I am in debt of others."

"But you didn't enthrone me, so I am in no debt to you. Yes, you brought me back to life, but that was your choice to make. Really, child, did you think I had any intention of doing any favours for you?" Zeus laughed. He waved her out, but Zara stood rigid.

"Do you expect me to accept that and leave?" she spat, her eyes flashing. "I owe others, and you owe me. I've gone through so much to bring you back, and in return you give me nothing, and expect me to be satisfied? Who do you think you are, you prestigious fool?!"

Zeus looked at her with contempt. "Leave. If that is how you are going to speak to your better, I do not want to hear any more."

Zara gritted her teeth, but Hades put his hand on her shoulder and steered her away. "Do not get mad at him, he is still bathing in the glory of being King again. Leave him to gloat over Poseidon."

The door slammed behind them. Zara glared at Hades. *How can this man be my father?* she thought angrily. *He has no sense of right and wrong! And how Zeus just treated me is wrong indeed!*

"You don't understand! I owe Hermes double his tips and some wings, and as well as I need to give all of Poseidon's guards a new job! If I do not give keep my promises, I will lose my powers, and my dignity!" Zara stormed.

Hades looked worried. "You swore an oath on your powers?"

"I treasure them the most. And I was so sure Zeus would give me such simple objects. I mean, that is within his power now that he owns the sceptre Hephaestus created from everyone's weapons." Zara sighed in frustration.

"But you swore an oath on your powers! You foolish child, as soon as you step out onto the clouds you shall fall through them, and your bones will shatter on the Earth's hard surface!" Hades thundered.

Zara winced and stepped away from him slightly. This could not go on. She needed to knock Zeus down a few pegs. She had not come all this way for nothing. Suddenly, a brilliant idea came to her.

"Excuse me a second." Zara turned back towards the unlocked door, kicked it open, stalked into the room and back over to Zeus.

She grabbed the sceptre by the hilt and tore it from Zeus's hands, much to his protest and anger. As she had hoped, the hilt began to sink into her palm, melting into her skin. The whole weapon would soon be gone, and become a part of her.

Zeus lunged forwards to grab her by the collar, but she leapt back lightly on her feet. Zeus was left clutching empty air.

The weapon was now completely absorbed under her skin. Zara smiled, put up her hand as Zeus charged forwards again and an invisible shield barred his way about three inches from her.

"Mmm," Zara hummed. "This is quite fun." She flexed her fingers, which were now shining a radiant white-blue. Zeus struggled to force his way past the barrier, but to no avail.

"Well, I will see you sometime. For now, I have some wishes to grant. Behave yourselves whilst I'm gone," Zara said cheerfully to Zeus and Poseidon, then turned on her heel and walked out of the room. The door had disappeared altogether, for there was now no proper key to fit the lock.

Hades looked annoyed with Zara. "You are disobedient."

"But this way, I can repay my debts, no one may rule the Gods and everyone is free to do as they please. I have done the right thing," Zara retorted. She waved her hand and a leather pouch of coins appeared. Two pairs of wings appeared, one plain white and feathery, another black and feathery with white patterns coursing through.

The black pair flapped over to her back, attaching themselves onto her jacket. The other flew straight into her hands, to which she attached the pouch of coins. She whispered to the wings and they set off, diving down and out the double doors.

"Now for the jobs for the guards. They've quit, anyhow, simply by disobeying their master. Be sure to tell Poseidon he's lost a few soldiers. See if you can tell them to make some sort of fast food section up here. Seriously, you guys are missing out," Zara said to Hades, then walked over to the ledge, about to jump off and fly down when he stopped her.

"Zara... why are you so dutiful? You seem to always think about everyone else before yourself. Why?" Hades asked.

Zara looked over her shoulder and smiled slyly. "I guess I was born that way, Father. You may want to start this habit yourself if you're going to cope with Mother telling you about me. By Mother I mean Persephone."

"What?" Hades cried, but Zara had already launched herself off the railing and sailed down to the floor.

He watched her bolt out the doors and onto the clouds, looking delighted and free. He scratched his head and turned around.

"Now, I think I might have to talk to Persephone about something here..."

CHAPTER FIFTEEN

Endings and Beginnings

Zara flew quietly out onto the clouds. She dared not land, in case she did fall through the clouds, because then there would be no way of getting back... at least that she knew of.

But now what was she to do? She had achieved her goal, and perhaps improved her plan slightly. Now everything was back to normal, and better. She had nothing to do now that her quest was complete.

She snapped her head to the right when she heard a bright bark, and saw Astra bounding across the clouds over to her side. He looked up at her and wagged his tail, his tongue lolling out of his mouth. He seemed content, and not nearly as depressed as he had been when Artemis had left.

Zara remembered Artemis. Was she still touring Earth, telling everyone Zeus was dead? That was not true anymore. She needed to inform Artemis that Zeus was alive, and he was ruling again. But what would Earth be like, and how would she find Artemis? Was Earth small, or completely endless? She had no idea about anything to do with this other realm.

Zara bent down and patted Astra's head, smiling thinly. *Well,* she thought, *we'll just have to see what comes! Another adventure between me, myself and I. And just who might I meet? And will I attain my goal? Who cares even? Perhaps it's just exploring that counts...*

Astra barked as she began to hover off without him. She turned to face him and smiled, a little sadly. "Stay up here and wait for me," she said sternly. "I promise that when I next visit, I will bear news of Artemis. Good or bad. I need you to stay here and wait. Okay?"

Astra growled, and looked away, but sat down obediently and bowed his head. "Good boy," Zara smiled wider, and ruffled his soft fur.

With that, she took a risk and fluttered down onto the clouds and bolted off in pursuit of an exit. Wherever that might be.

She didn't know, but she would soon find out.

Afterword

I tip my hat to you, dear Reader, for picking up and reading this book. It's taken longer than expected to bring this book to you, but every time I look back at it, it's satisfying to see how far I've come.

Big thanks to my Dad - my manager, my kind-of editor and critic. Thank you for being my Dad throughout this, not some sort of stiff person who just points out mistakes. You were there to help me improve, not correct me (and there is a difference).

Thanks to Stephanie, who edited my book and showed me that there was so much more to my writing that I need to look out for. It really opened my eyes and when I write now I keep in mind the past, present and future of the book. Never forget a character, never forget a reference - it all adds up at some point, and if it doesn't, it doesn't make sense. That is an amazingly important lesson and you couldn't have taught it better.

Thanks to Skye for being inspiring. I only met her once, and usually I just would have thought of her as a friend of a relative, but it really felt like I saw more than a person there. Something amazing that would motivate me through the years - someone who can read, write, and change the world as much as I can. So thanks, Skye, for being you - and that's so much more than meets the eye.

For those of you wanting more, know that this is just the beginning. I have lofty goals, and to every one of you willing to come along for the ride, buckle up and get ready.

You never know what I'm going to do next.

Also by Skye Lotus

<u>Starry Wings Saga</u>
Sweet Dreams, Not!
Frozen to the spot
Dancing flames
Zombies Ahead
Crown Hunters

available as eBooks from
all good eBook stores.

Visit

www.skyelotus.com

for more of Skye's writings, or find her on
goodreads.com

www.ingramcontent.com/pod-product-compliance
Lightning Source LLC
Chambersburg PA
CBHW021201110726

47900CB00002B/684